For parents and other secret Santas everywhere
whose hidden fear whispers,
"Is it enough? Will the gifts be acceptable?"

❧ PREFACE ❧

The Great Depression that followed the 1929 stock-market crash stretched for more than a decade, ending only with World War II. Many families lost their homes; some never really recovered from the economic devastation. That terrible era was indeed a desperate time. It also spawned acts of quiet, anonymous generosity as well as remarkable, truly inspiring examples of the indomitable human spirit. Although *Secret Santa* is fiction, its basic theme is true. The core of the story is derived from an incident in my husband's childhood. Tom van Sloten shares many of Ron's personal characteristics; however, Tom is imaginary, as are the rest of his family members.

Some of the characters depicted here are real. A few of Tom's teachers—J. Hazel Whitcomb, Lisle Bradford, and Phyllis Tregagle—actually taught at East High School (although the story is set a decade earlier for dramatic purposes). The remainder of the East High faculty and administration are fictitious. Joe and Evelyn Rosenblatt are real, as is Joe's account of his father's emigrating from Russia. Rosenblatt's Department Store is imaginary. On the other hand, Sam Weller and his famous Zion Book Store (one of the last great independent bookstores in the United States) are real.

I am indebted to my husband, Ronald E. Poelman, for his vivid retelling of his memories from the Great Depression. Thanks to Annie Hinckley for her historical research. The few anachronisms that exist in *Secret Santa* are mine, not hers, and have been used deliberately for dramatic effect. Judge Regnal Garff, longtime justice of the juvenile court, was an invaluable source of information regarding the treatment of young offenders in the court's early days. "Jeannie's" Christmas Eve poem was written by my late sister-in-law, Carol Poelman Feltch; thanks to her husband, Brent, for permitting me to use it. Richard Paul Evans, author of *The Christmas Box*, was a great example as well as a wonderful source of advice and encouragement. I appreciate the patience and valuable input of editors Tim Robinson and Emily Watts. *Secret Santa* reflects their consummate skill at helping authors make their stories even better.

Finally, thanks to you, the reader. It is for you that we tell this story. If it inspires anyone to be a little better, to behave more kindly, or to share more generously, it will have filled the measure of its existence.

Anne Osborn Poelman
Salt Lake City, Utah

❧ CHAPTER ONE ❧
Monday afternoon, December 11, 1933

He did not enjoy being a child. Decades later, when he had children and grandchildren of his own, he realized he had spent most of his first sixteen years of life struggling to become an adult. Hard-won experience had taught him that adulthood, once such a desirable status, just meant trading one set of anxieties and responsibilities for another.

For now, he was simply trying to survive adolescence.

He lived in a constant state of anxiety. An eager and conscientious student, he worried about grades as he pored over his homework. He wanted to be liked, not just respected for his academic prowess. He yearned to be part of a "crowd." Not even the In Crowd; *any* crowd would do. He was self-conscious about his unfashionable clothes, warm-weather hand-me-downs that were both out of date and out of season in the harsh Utah winter. To him, they screamed "Square!" And to be square was worse than being dead.

A summer growth spurt shot his height over six feet. Although this newfound stature pleased him mightily, it meant all his pants were too short. "Expecting a flood?" his classmates teased.

Sometimes he stared at his reflection in the bathroom mirror, turning this way and that as he critically examined every feature. With its high cheekbones and jutting aquiline nose, his face seemed all sharp angles slapped together like some abstract painting. He dreamed that by an unexpected miracle a cute girl might find him attractive.

His shy smile exposed the space left by a missing tooth. When the molar had first started to ache, he had poked cotton balls dipped in oil of clove into the deep cavity he had discovered was eroding the tooth. When that home remedy no longer killed the pain, he searched the newspaper to find the least expensive dentist. A Doctor J. G. Davies advertised silver fillings at $1, with porcelain fillings ranging from $1.50 to $2.50. He called the office and took the first available appointment. When Dr. Davies told him it would be cheaper to pull the tooth than fill it, the tooth had to go. The extra fifty cents the dentist charged for anesthesia was an indulgence he couldn't afford.

He rubbed his jaw at the uncomfortable memory. He had learned to disguise the unsightly gap with a lopsided grin, but because his sister said it made him look "goofy," he rarely smiled.

He was even sensitive about his odd name. "What kind of a name is *that?*" a thoughtless teacher had once asked after mangling the pronunciation. "It's Dutch. It means 'from the stream,'" he had mumbled, embarrassed that he didn't have a simple but famous local name like Young or Kimball or Cannon.

In short, Tom van Sloten was a normal teenager. At least he would have been, had he grown up in normal times. But the depths of the Great Depression were hardly normal.

Following the disastrous 1929 stock market crash, the Depression was an economic tidal wave that inundated the world. Historians describe that terrible era in technical terms as a worldwide "loss of liquidity." To young Tom van Sloten, it seemed as though a giant vacuum cleaner had sucked up all the world's money. The Depression transformed rich into poor and made the poor—the van Slotens among them—destitute.

On his way to his own after-school job, Tom had often observed dispirited people waiting for hours in silent, shared misery for a bowl of thin soup and a slice of coarse bread. The employment lines always formed long before dawn and snaked around entire city blocks, filled with silent men hoping for a day's work. His own father, a first-generation Dutch-Scottish immigrant with only a high school education, was often among them.

Home from work, Tom arranged his textbooks on the old gate-legged table in the corner of the cramped living room, hoping to steal a few minutes of precious study time before dinner. He wondered for the umpteenth time what arcane custom kept the dining room off-limits, unused except on Sundays or special occasions. It was one of only four rooms in their drafty rented house.

Trying to ignore the shouts and squeals of his younger brothers as they surged around the small living room and spilled into the kitchen, Tom puzzled out a difficult introductory calculus problem for extra credit.

The front door banged open as his sister Jean burst into the room, accompanied by a blast of frigid air. "I'm home!" she announced, pulling off her knit cap with a sweeping gesture aimed at an invisible audience. Her thick chestnut hair tumbled out, cascading down to her shoulders.

Jean's mouth tightened as she spied Tom in his customary spot, hunched over his books. Engrossed in his studies, he was oblivious to her dramatic entrance.

She cleared her throat, harrumphing loudly.

Tom glanced up and sighed. How did she do it? Somehow his sister *always* managed to look fashionable, even glamorous. She could rummage around in a trunk of old clothes at a secondhand store, pick out something inexpensive—quite ordinary, really—and with a deft touch transform it into a stylish outfit. Jean was immensely popular and had already attracted the attention of older boys—much to her delight and her parents' dismay. Just that day, one of Tom's own classmates had whispered a plea to "fix him up" with her. When he weakly protested that she was only fifteen, the classmate had smirked and shot him a knowing wink.

Jean strode across the room, dodging the younger boys as she planted herself squarely in front of Tom. She leaned over and flipped his notebook closed to insure his undivided attention. "Well, if it isn't Mr. Perfect!" she smirked. "Every teacher's pet!"

Lowering her face within inches of his, Jean stared at him. A concerned frown suddenly replaced her mocking smile. "Oh!" she inhaled with a little gasp of alarm as her hand flew to her mouth. She bit her knuckle in dismay as she leaned even closer. "Oh, Tom!" she exclaimed in an ominous tone. "There's a black spot right on the end of your nose. I just read about those in biology class. Maybe it's a malignant mole!"

Tom shot out of his chair and raced to the tiny bathroom, peering at himself in the mirror.

"I don't see anything, Jeannie," he replied, turning back to his sister with a worried look.

"Uh-huh," she nodded sagely as she examined his face again. "It's there, all right." She tapped the end of his nose. "It's really small. But I was mistaken. It's not a black mole after all; it's just some ink. From keeping your nose stuck in books all the time!"

She guffawed at her own joke. Baiting Tom was so easy it hardly seemed fair.

Then Jean hissed at him in a loud stage whisper: "Listen to me, Thomas van Sloten! I'm serious about this. *Really* serious! If I hear one more teacher say one more time, 'Jean, why can't you just apply yourself like your brother Tom,' I'll scream! I swear I will!"

"Jeannie! We don't swear in this house," their mother warned, overhearing the interchange from the kitchen. "You've picked up some pretty salty language, young lady, though goodness only knows where. You certainly don't hear swearing in *this* household. Come and do something useful, like helping with supper," she ordered, pointing with her chin toward the sink.

Jean grimaced.

"I'm sorry, Jeannie," Tom muttered miserably, trying without success to mollify his sister. He wondered what he did that seemed to annoy her on such a regular basis. Some days it seemed as though his very existence offended her. He knew she loved him; what he really wanted was for her to *like* him, even a little bit. She was only a year younger, but because he had skipped a grade, he was two years ahead of her in school. Maybe that was what made him a target for her special scorn.

People marveled at how beautiful and charming Jean was. Everyone liked her. Children adored her, and her thriving baby-sitting business was the envy of her many girlfriends. Rumor had it that even in these cash-strapped times, some of her clients were offering bonuses and free meals to attract her services. She did have a special way with people, he conceded. Even animals were drawn to her.

Tom thought back a few months, recalling the first warm day of spring. It was a holiday, so his parents had taken the younger children to the park. As usual, he had elected to stay home and study. He had allowed himself the luxury of a brief break, stretching and resting his eyes for a few delicious moments. Looking out the living-room window, he was surprised to see Jean. She had returned from a morning of baby-sitting and was perched on the front steps, enjoying the solitude. The brilliant sun filtered through the trees, limning her with gold like a backlit madonna. She was munching on the remains of a peanut butter and jelly sandwich, eyes closed and face turned upward as she basked in the welcome warmth.

Tom swallowed, mouth watering. Peanut butter and jelly was a rare treat. His favorite.

A small squirrel, gaunt from winter hibernation, crawled down one of the large trees that bordered the street and began a frantic foraging in the yard. Tom saw his sister open her eyes, apparently sensing its presence. A smile crept across her face as she slowly unwrapped the crusts, all that remained of her sack lunch. She held out a morsel to the squirrel. It startled in alarm, then took a hesitant step toward her. Its flanks rippled with tension.

Jean's lips moved. He realized she was speaking to the frightened animal in that low, compelling voice of hers, soothing and enticing it. It took another step toward her, then another, quivering with indecision.

What happened next astonished him.

The squirrel was within a few inches of Jean's outstretched hand. Overcoming its natural fear, it hesitantly took the bread. But instead of seizing its prize and dashing to safety, it scampered up her leg. Crouching in her lap, it calmly chewed the crust until the last crumbs had been devoured. Then the tiny thing sat there as Jean lightly stroked its fur, murmuring words of encouragement. The squirrel's eyes drooped in contentment.

After a few extraordinary minutes, Jean placed the squirrel on the ground and gently shooed it off. It dashed up the nearest tree and perched on a lower branch, squeaking and chattering at her. Tom could almost imagine it saying, "Hey! Thanks for the snack!"

Why can't she work some of that magic on me, her own brother? he wondered, envying the squirrel.

Tom's wistful musings were interrupted by a high-pitched shout. "Daddy's coming!" little David squealed as he flattened his nose against the living-room window and watched his breath condense against the icy glass.

Tom moved to the window, hoisting David to his shoulders as his youngest brother wriggled with delight. They both peered into the dusk at a stooped figure who rounded the corner and paused, leaning against a street-light for temporary support.

It was their father, Hendrik. The harsh light drained all the color from his pale skin, making it seem even more sallow than usual. He was panting. Tom stiffened as Hendrik clutched his heaving chest, face contorted with pain.

"Tommy!" David grabbed his brother's shirt in alarm. "What's wrong with Daddy?"

"He's okay, Davey," Tom replied, feigning an assurance he didn't feel. "I think Dad's just tired."

Hendrik had walked the three miles home again. At five cents a token, taking the streetcar was a rare indulgence. A few years ago, in more promising times, he had moved his family from an even smaller house in a working-class neighborhood on the city's west side. Hendrik often joked that their former home was "not just on the wrong side of the railroad tracks but *in between* two sets of tracks." He had wanted his children to attend East High School, renowned for its college preparatory classes.

As the Depression ground on, the bold move now seemed like a rash gamble, a decision somehow gone terribly wrong.

As his breathing eased, Hendrik shuffled down the sidewalk.

He's not even forty and he looks like an old man, Tom fretted in his mind. He watched as his father stopped again before climbing the rickety steps to their front porch. Hendrik ran gnarled fingers through his graying hair. Then, with visible effort, he pulled his face into a cheery smile.

David clambered down and ran to the door, yanking it open and screeching with delight, "Daddy!"

"Sarah!" Hendrik exclaimed to his wife as he rubbed his arms, trying to banish the ache in his left shoulder that was traveling all the way down to his wrist. "A good day, today was!"

David wrapped his slight body around his father's bony leg. Hendrik gathered his son in his arms and lowered himself onto the worn sofa, pulling off the heavy, oversized boots that he stuffed with old newspapers each morning for added insulation.

"Whew!" he sighed with relief as he rubbed his swollen feet. "I got real lucky today. The city foreman—a guy I used to work with at the old roofing company—pulled me out of the job line before dawn. Sent me with his emergency crew to repair a leaking water line. The city pays five cents an hour more than everybody else, so I made nearly three dollars today!"

"It was a good day for me too, Dad. Mrs. Whitcomb gave me an A on my American history term paper!" Tom reported. "She wrote 'very nice work' on it, too."

Hendrik smiled with pride.

"It was a good day all the way around," Sarah put in as the younger children clambered onto the couch, surrounding their father and all chattering at once. "We made popcorn balls. Richard and Paul sold nearly three dozen at two for a nickel."

"Look, Dad!" the two boys exclaimed proudly as they displayed their earnings. "Almost a whole dollar!"

"Well, now, aren't you the clever ones!" Hendrik beamed.

"The children made some extras and took them to shut-ins and widows," Sarah added. "It isn't much, but small acts of kindness can make such a difference these days."

Hendrik pulled the rumpled bills and loose coins out of his pocket. Richard and Paul added their contributions as Sarah stacked the coins next to the worrisome pile of unpaid bills on the narrow kitchen counter. "Three dollars and ninety cents," she announced. "First things first. That's the Lord's share." She counted out thirty-nine cents and placed the money in a special envelope reserved for church contributions. She hesitated, then added another dime. "Plus ten cents as alms for the poor," she concluded.

"Mom!" Jean protested. "*We're* the poor!"

"No, Jeannie," Sarah corrected her in a mild voice. "We're rich. At least in the things that really matter."

Jean looked dubious. It wasn't the first time she'd heard *that* particular line. Hendrik put his arm around his only daughter. "Mother's right. We have each other. We have the church. Making our contributions and helping the poor—the *really* poor—is a privilege, not a burden."

"I'm hungry!" David complained to chuckles from the rest of the family.

Sarah laughed as the focus shifted from philosophical concerns to more immediate ones. She unwrapped a white slab of oleomargarine and sprinkled it with a packet of powdered yellow food coloring, gradually working the artificial color into the congealed fat until it resembled softened butter. Then she scraped a stack of diced potatoes into a large cast-iron skillet that was heating on the old coal-burning stove. Hot grease popped and sizzled as she added a generous handful of onions along with salt and a dash of pepper. She thought for a moment, then pulled a tin of corned beef from the nearly empty cupboard.

"A special day means a special dinner. *Real* corned beef hash tonight!" she announced. Tom gathered up his books so Jean could set the table. Everyone crowded onto the sturdy benches that substituted for chairs, bowing their heads as Hendrik offered a prayer of thanksgiving. "Amen!" the family chorused with gratitude for the day's successes. Sarah portioned out the hash and passed around a large loaf of homemade bread. Each child spread a thin layer of the cheap margarine over the thick slices, scraping off any excess and putting it back in the crock.

"Jam?" Tom queried hopefully. Sarah shook her head. One treat was enough.

After dinner, the table was cleared and converted back into a study desk as the children concentrated on their homework. As usual, Jean finished first.

A loud "brrring, *brring*, BRRIINNGG!!" erupted from the telephone, a four-party line the family shared with their neighbors. Three rings meant the call was for the van Slotens. Jean raced to the phone and snatched the receiver from its cradle on the wall before anyone else could react.

"This is WAsatch 2261," she said in a low, honeyed voice. "Jean van Sloten speaking. May I help you?"

She fell silent for a moment, listening intently.

"Oh," she said, expectant tone vanishing. "Yes, he is. He's right here." Her lips pursed into a tight circle as she covered the mouthpiece with her hand. "Tom, it's for *you!* It's Mrs. Whitcomb. She wants to talk to you."

Tom was stunned. He'd never heard of a teacher calling a student at home. He jumped up, knocking the bench over and sending his younger brothers flying. "This—this is Tom, Mrs. Whitcomb. Ma'am," he added, stammering.

The family listened, determined to catch every word and nuance of this unprecedented event.

"Uh, thank you, Mrs. Whitcomb. Yes, I did enjoy writing the essay." He paused, then shook his head. "A radio? Yes, of course we have one." Another pause. "No, it's not on right now. I, uh—we're, uh, studying." He hated to tell his revered teacher the whole truth, that the old console radio had been broken for months and there was no money for repairs.

"The BBC?" A blast of static on the line disrupted the call. "What? I'm sorry, could you say that again, please?" Tom apologized. "Oh. Yes, Mrs. Whitcomb. I'll try to catch it next week," he promised. He nodded to himself as she continued. Then he started in surprise as Mrs. Whitcomb conveyed the rest of her news. "A new scholarship? Yes, ma'am, of course I'll think about applying. Thanks, Mrs. Whitcomb. See you tomorrow."

Tom hung up, hope etched on his face. "That was Mrs. Whitcomb. *The* Mrs. Whitcomb!" he exclaimed. "There's a new history scholarship at the university she thinks I might have a shot at. And she wants me to write a term paper next semester on Hitler and American isolationism!"

"Well, *I'm* going to 'isolate' myself right into bed," Jean declared, trying to appear unimpressed. Rolling up in a quilt on the living-room sofa, she was asleep within minutes.

Sarah shooed the younger children toward the boys' "bedroom," in reality a screened-in back porch with two bunk beds. In the summer it was fun. In winter, sleeping there was a test of character.

Hendrik banked the fire in the coal stove and put a large lump in the living-room fireplace. In a daily ritual that never ceased to delight the children, he would arise in the morning, take a poker, and split the smoldering lump with a single firm tap that would have done an Amsterdam diamond cutter proud. The lump always shattered in a spectacular shower of glowing embers, suffusing the chilly house with warmth.

Tasks done, Hendrik stood in the kitchen and stared at the stack of unpaid bills. The coal bill had reached the critical stage. Their landlord, short of cash himself, was pressing for the long-overdue rent.

Holidays were always an especially anxious time, but tonight Hendrik felt a special sense of desperation. Christmas was only two weeks away. Even before the Depression had robbed him of steady work, he had felt every parent's hidden fear. Would the meager, practical gifts be enough? Would the children be pleased? Or would they rip through the sparse packages, looking at him with faces twisted in disappointment?

This year the phrase *joy of Christmas* seemed like a cruel joke. In better times, a gaily decorated tree had stood tall and proud in the living room. Today the traditional spot was bare, a stark reminder of their poverty.

Cold air seeped through the poorly insulated windows, diluting the tiny home's warmth and dampening Hendrik's mood. In a world where a man's worth was defined by his strength as a good provider, he felt helpless and inadequate as a father. He watched in silence as Sarah resumed the financial activity that had been interrupted by supper. Dividing the remaining money between two envelopes, she reported, "Here are the coal and electricity bills." Tom would deliver the payments on his way to work after school the next day. Each hand-delivered envelope saved a precious three-cent stamp.

"Sarah," Hendrik said slowly, "I don't see any way there can be much of a Christmas this year. The money just isn't there. We won't even have a tree." He sank his face into his hands. Hot tears of shame ran down his cheeks, trickling through wrinkles that worry had etched into canyons.

Sarah buried her head on her husband's shoulder, struggling to control her own despair. "Not everything costs money, Henry. We can still read the scriptures together. Sing carols. Visit friends. After all, those—and our love for each other and the children—are the most important things." Losing the battle with her emotions, she let out a stifled sob.

Tom's head jerked up at the sound. He craned his neck, peering around the corner into the kitchen. Hendrik and Sarah were staring at the remaining stack of bills, faces tear-stained. "Friday is payday, Dad," he reminded his father. "That can take care of a few more of those."

Hendrik shook his head as he shuffled past the table and wearily headed toward the bedroom. "You need that money for college, Tom. Maybe things will look brighter in the morning." He smiled weakly. "Who knows? I might even be lucky two days in a row. I'll get up and make it to the job line even earlier than usual. That might make my chances a little better."

"You seem to sleep better when you prop yourself up a bit," Sarah observed. "So I borrowed an extra pillow from the neighbors. That should help."

Tom turned back to his schoolbooks, digging in to study for a chemistry test. Sarah settled down at their old treadle-powered sewing machine to remodel a shirt an older cousin had given Richard. The rhythmic clack and hum of the machine, a comforting, homey sound that Tom loved, soon filled the small room.

Sarah's hands flew as she expertly guided the material under the flashing needle, turning the new seams and snipping loose threads. She finally held up the finished garment and smiled with satisfaction. Richard would be pleased. She carefully folded the new-old shirt and left it on the table where he would find it in the morning.

"Good night, son," Sarah said, kissing Tom gently on the forehead. "I'm proud of you. Things will work out. Somehow."

Sometime after midnight, Tom closed the chemistry book and headed for bed. He stripped off his school clothes in the kitchen and donned a pair of worn pajamas. Bracing himself, he jerked open the door to the sleeping porch and dived into the bunk. With an involuntary gasp at the shock of cold sheets on bare skin, Tom pulled the heavy pile of blankets up to his chin and lay there shivering. His breath curled into the air in silvery puffs.

As his body heat gradually warmed the blankets, his breathing slowed and Tom could focus on something other than his own discomfort. "Thank you, Lord," he prayed silently. "Thanks for Christmas and what it means. For our family. For our many blessings. But why does it have to be such a struggle? I know you often slept outside too. But was Palestine ever as cold as Salt Lake City in the winter?"

❧ CHAPTER TWO ❧
Early Tuesday morning, December 12, 1933

T om woke up with a start, mouth too dry to swallow. His heart was pounding, slamming against his ribs so hard he thought his chest would explode. Despite the below-freezing temperature on the sleeping porch, he was drenched with sour sweat. During the night snow had drifted in through the loosely shuttered screens and dusted his bed with a fine white frost. As he tried to remember what had frightened him so badly, remnants of a terrifying nightmare surfaced and then retreated, lingering just beyond the edge of recall.

With effort he rolled over beneath the heavy blankets and squinted at the old windup clock. Its luminous dial glowed in the pitch dark. He groaned. *Two-thirty in the morning!* He had set the alarm for 3:30 A.M., his usual time to get up for his job at Dunford's Bakery. Desperate for rest, he tried in vain to get back to sleep, tossing and turning until the clock's harsh ring roused him for the day. Shivering in the cold, he slipped into his clothes and pulled on the thin cotton jacket that served as his winter coat. He made himself a cup of Postum and downed it in quick gulps, then dashed out the door to the neighborhood bakery.

Bill and Bob Dunford greeted Tom with their customary cheer as he ran into the shop and grabbed his apron from its wooden peg. He stood in the heat radiating from the giant ovens until he stopped shaking from the cold, then began forming the dough the Dunfords had made into fat, oblong loaves.

As the mounds of dough rose and pushed their way out of the pans, the Dunfords misted the tops with warm water so the loaves would form a thick, chewy crust as they baked. Tom helped the brothers position the racks of bulging dough in the great ovens. The bread would be baked, cooled, sliced, and wrapped long before dawn. On Saturdays Tom sometimes worked an extra two hours delivering the fresh loaves to nearby grocery stores. On weekdays he always ran home to gulp down a quick breakfast prior to leaving again for school.

"Hey, Tom!" one of the brothers called to him just as he headed out the door. "Almost forgot. I got somethin' for you!" He reached under the counter and extended a waxed paper bag toward Tom. Tom peeked inside. The bag was filled with Dunford's famous chocolate doughnuts! "We had a few of these left when we closed up yesterday afternoon," Bill Dunford explained. Tom raised a quizzical eyebrow. Even in the depths of the Depression, Dunford's Bakery *always* sold out its daily inventory of chocolate doughnuts.

"Take it," Bob urged as he pressed the bag into Tom's hands. "I'm tired of 'em, myself. My wife says I shouldn't eat so many anyway," he grinned as he patted his protruding belly.

"Somehow we think you can help 'em 'fill the measure of their creation,' so to speak," Bill concurred with a wink as Tom thanked them for their generosity and dashed out the door.

He was ecstatic. Breakfast in the van Sloten home was always the same: stale bread toasted and then softened with milk. Cracked wheat—simmered overnight in a tightly covered pot—or steamed oatmeal substituted for costly prepared cereals such as Wheaties. Sometimes as a treat they would have bottled fruit that the family had canned in the summer when supplies were plentiful and cheap. But chocolate doughnuts? Tom crowed with elation. *Wait'll the kids see this!*

Tom's lighthearted run slowed to a walk. He had just remembered the nightmare, an ugly dream that seemed to recur during especially stressful times. It was always the same. In the dream he saw himself as a new freshman at the University of Utah, standing in a long line to register for his first quarter of classes. The line moved at a glacial pace, filled with well-dressed students who all seemed to know each other as they talked and joked in an easy, confident manner.

The students ignored him. They looked through him, past him, beyond him as though he didn't exist. Their excited chatter reverberated in the cavernous building, hurting his ears.

Finally it was his turn at the window. A stern-faced registrar, hair pulled back in a severe bun, peered at him. "Name?" she asked in a curt voice.

"Van Sloten. Thomas van Sloten," he stammered.

"Spell it," she ordered. Much to his embarrassment, he had to repeat it three times before she got it right. "Small *v*, capital *S*, with a space in between." The other students, no longer oblivious to his presence, snickered at the odd name. Even in the dream he could feel his face flush scarlet.

"Classes?" the registrar queried. He handed over a list of his choices.

She gave the sheet a cursory glance. "Sorry, they're all full," she said, shaking her head as she pushed the list back, clearly not sorry at all.

"But I *have* to have those classes," Tom protested. "They're required! How can they be full?"

"You'll have to choose other ones," she shrugged, indifferent to his plight. "Step out of line and fill out a new list." Waving him aside, the registrar gestured to an attractive girl waiting impatiently behind Tom and called, "*Next!*"

The girl seemed vaguely familiar, but Tom couldn't remember how or why he knew her. She brushed past him, making small talk with the registrar, who was suddenly all smiles and gracious nods. "Oh, Eliza Gates Cannon. I know your family, Miss Cannon, wonderful people," the registrar added with an obsequious dip of her head.

A chime echoed in the distance. "Registration will close in half an hour," a hidden voice announced in sepulchral tones.

Tom felt a surge of panic as he rushed to fill out a list of his second choices, hastily consulting the course catalog. Knowing what invariably came next, he always tried to struggle into consciousness and wrench himself from the dream's nightmarish grip. He rarely succeeded.

The registration line moved even more sluggishly. The other students milled around, catching up on the summer's gossip and consulting each other about last-minute schedule changes. He caught snatches of conversation, clipped phrases that seemed to ricochet around his whirling brain.

"She's dating *Bill?* You've got to be kidding! What in the world does he see in *her?*"

"I think Barbara'll probably pledge Chi O."

"They'll never rush her, not in a million years."

"Too bad he's a West High guy."

"Well, *I* think he's cute! And he has a car!"

At last it was Tom's turn again. He passed his revised list to the registrar. She scanned it as she absently pressed a rubber stamp into a red inkpad. Then, with an authoritative thump, she stamped his classes "approved."

"Tuition is $20.00 for lower division students, with a quarterly class fee of seventy-five cents," she droned in a bored monotone as she began entering figures on an adding machine. "An annual registration fee of $10.00 is required of all resident students and is payable at the time of registration. That's now, of course. The Union Building fee is $3.00. General student body activity fee is $9.25. There's a health examination fee of $1.00 that is required of all first-time students. That's you. The towel fee is also $1.00. Deposit for a towel tag—refundable, of course, *if* and when you turn the towel in—is fifty cents. That'll be a total of $45.50, payable at the cashier's window. Down the hall on the right."

Tom sighed with relief. He would have enough, just barely. He pulled from his pocket the worn leather pouch that contained his life's savings.

It was empty. He turned it upside down and shook it in disbelief. Nothing fell out. Panic-stricken, he plunged his hands into his pockets, searching frantically. He found only a half-stick of Wrigley's gum in its silver wrapper and a few small bits of lint.

He broke out in a cold sweat. "I, I—it was *here*, I swear it!" he almost shouted as he looked around in despair.

The other students started pointing at him and laughing.

"Guy's got a nerve! Thinks he can be up here on the hill *for free!*"

"Look at him! Look at his clothes! Have you *ever* in all your born days seen such a getup?"

"Square!"

"He's got to be an Alpha Sigma Sigma!" a fraternity man in an immaculate varsity letter sweater sneered, pleased at his own wit.

The registrar slammed down the window and turned over a sign. *Closed to Thomas van Sloten. This means* **you**, it read.

The jeering students circled Tom. He spun and whirled like a cornered animal. Pushing his way through the ring, he tried to flee the building, taunts and derisive shouts pursuing him like a pack of hunting dogs. Tom's legs felt like lead as he forced himself toward an exit that seemed to keep shrinking as it moved impossibly far away. He felt as if he were running through molasses, feet barely moving.

With a last, desperate plunge he finally burst through the door . . .

. . . and found himself wide awake, standing on the sidewalk in front of the van Sloten home. He was sweating profusely. Tom shivered, knowing it wasn't the early morning chill that was making him shake.

Sarah van Sloten, mouth stuffed with clothespins, looked up as Tom came through the front door and closed it with a bang. He leaned against the door, white-faced and trembling.

"Tom!" Sarah exclaimed as she stopped hanging wet clothes from the wires that ringed the walls of the van Slotens' living and dining rooms. "You look as if you've just seen a ghost! What happened?"

Tom shook his head, trying to clear his dazed brain. "Nothing. Really," he mumbled. "I'm just—tired. I think I stayed up too late studying chemistry last night. I'll be okay."

Jean, stuffing a last spoonful of oatmeal into her mouth, spied the Dunford's bag. She jumped up and snatched it from Tom's unresisting grasp. "Doughnuts!" she shouted with glee as she peeked in the sack. "Chocolate ones, too!"

"Not for breakfast, Jeannie." Sarah took the bag and put it in the barren kitchen cupboard. "We'll have them for dinner tonight."

Jean pouted but didn't dare protest. Sarah's sharp glance brooked no argument. "Run along, now. Don't be late for school again," she admonished, knowing Jean had accumulated a string of unexcused tardy notices. Jean grabbed her books, made a face at Tom when Sarah wasn't looking, and flounced out the door.

Sarah spooned a large helping of oatmeal into a bowl and handed it to Tom. Then she added a bit of brown sugar and a dollop of the cream she had skimmed from the top of the milk bottle and saved for treats. "You look as if you could use some extra energy," she said, her voice heavy with concern.

"I'm all right," Tom insisted as he toyed with his spoon. He didn't feel very hungry.

"You need to eat," Sarah ordered. "You seem so—well, I guess maybe *distracted*."

The nightmare's horror was too fresh, too raw to share. Tom finished his breakfast in silence, thanked his mother as he washed the dish and put it in the rack by the sink, and left to change into his school clothes.

The sleeping porch was empty, so quiet it seemed almost eerie. Each bunk bed was made, blankets turned under the thin mattresses in sharp, orderly corners. Tom had to smile. His mother ran a tight ship, all right. Even the younger boys hung up their clothes and put away their few belongings without being asked.

Tom opened his personal drawer in the battered dresser that he shared with his three brothers. He exhaled, weak with relief. The glass jar that served as his bank was stuffed with coins and dollar bills. The nightmare had been just that—only a bad dream, a figment of his overwrought imagination.

He'd tapped the jar for one emergency or another but had always managed to replenish it. The trip to the dentist to have his aching tooth pulled had put a temporary dent in his savings. Then there was the Sunday when Paul tripped on the broken concrete in front of their house, gashing his knee and ripping his only good pair of pants. Predictably, the family crisis had been the pants, not the knee. The knee would heal in time. The pants, torn beyond even his mother's uncanny ability to patch and repair, were the real disaster. The next day Tom dipped into the jar and bought his distraught little brother a brand-new pair.

Now he was finally making some headway, the jar once again brimming with coins and bills. Maybe he should at least consider . . . he shook his head. No. Absolutely not. He needed to stay focused on his long-term goal, attending the university. After all, he reassured himself, if he could just get a college education he would be in a much better position to help his family. One Christmas more or less surely wouldn't matter much in the overall scheme of things. Years later, who would remember a particular Christmas? The spartan Christmases he could recall were all pretty much the same anyway.

Feeling better, he put the jar back in his dresser drawer. Then he pulled out his greatest treasure, a small velvet box that contained a fine uncirculated "half eagle" five-dollar gold piece. He had won it in a statewide American Legion essay contest when he was at Roosevelt Junior High. The first prize of twenty-five dollars had been awarded to a senior girl from East High. Tom had won the second prize, astonishing everyone. He was the youngest prizewinner in the history of the contest. The topic, "Why America Is the World's Greatest Democracy," had fascinated him. His research in the public library had led him to the conclusion that America isn't a democracy at all. He thought the essay proved his point, that the United States is actually a republic, quite convincingly. He'd always secretly wondered if a more conventional approach would have given him a shot at the big prize.

His envious classmates had admired the gleaming coin, pestering him without mercy. "Wha'cha gonna spend it on?" they all clamored. He never told anyone, but he hadn't spent it on anything. Instead, right after the awards ceremony he had buttoned the little box securely in his pants pocket, hopped on his bicycle, and pedaled downtown to Delaney's Coin Shop.

Tom smiled, remembering the look on Mr. Delaney's face when he had placed the box on the counter and opened it.

Mr. Delaney gave a low whistle. "A 1908 gold piece. Mint condition, too," he breathed reverently.

"What's it worth, Mr. Delaney?" Tom had asked.

"Right now, no more than five dollars—its actual face value. But 1908 was the last year the government minted those half eagles. Your coin is uncirculated. That means it's in especially fine condition. You keep it a few years and I can guarantee you someday it'll be worth a lot more than that."

Tom put the box back in his pocket. "Thanks, Mr. Delaney. That's just what I needed to know. I'm going to keep it, maybe forever."

The old man nodded his approbation. "If you ever want to sell it, come see me. I'll guarantee you the best price you'll get anywhere. But if you want my advice, hold on to it. Gold is forever, you know."

Tom had kept the coin, stubbornly refusing to part with it even when times got truly desperate. Over the years it became his personal talisman. Its head, bearing the 1908 date, profiled a female figure surrounded by a ring of thirteen stars. Tom liked the flip side even better. It portrayed a magnificent eagle with outstretched wings, an oak branch and two arrows clutched in its long talons. The eagle's piercing scowl seemed to mirror his own fierce determination to succeed, no matter what it took.

Tom shot a last look at the eagle and closed the box, putting it back into the drawer next to the jar.

That's where it belonged. And that's where it would stay.

❧ CHAPTER THREE ❧
Tuesday afternoon, December 12, 1933

Major Garrison, Dean of Boys at East High School, paused at the door of the teachers' lounge. The real center of East wasn't the main-floor suite of administrative offices with its imposing phalanx of secretaries. He had to admit that the living, beating heart of the school was this small room, tucked into an obscure corner on the third floor. It was the teachers' sacrosanct domain, strictly off-limits to students.

Several years earlier, the faculty had begged the administration to let them make a musty, unused storeroom into a lounge. In what Garrison regarded as a fatal moment of weakness, the principal had supported their request. The school board had approved the concept but hadn't allocated funds for the makeover. Undeterred, the teachers had gradually transformed the room into a cozy, inviting meeting place. They furnished it themselves, assembling a collection of unmatched chairs and a discarded horsehide sofa. The walls, painted a nondescript institutional green, were covered with an eclectic display of art prints, posters, and pennants from the state's major colleges and universities. A folding table held a battered coffee urn along with a two-burner hotplate that the faculty used to heat water for Ovaltine and cocoa.

Garrison usually avoided the place like the plague, regarding the popular gathering spot as subversive.

"Major Garrison!" Jim Siddons, head of the math department, greeted him as he entered the crowded room. Garrison grimaced. He thought Siddons, the longest tenured teacher at East High, who also served as the faculty's unelected but de facto leader, was a closet rebel.

Siddons's faintly insubordinate tone made Garrison grit his teeth. He much preferred to be addressed as *Dean* Garrison. Or Mister Garrison. Or even Buck, his old childhood nickname. Why on earth his parents had chosen such fanciful names for their children was beyond understanding. Maybe their middle-class hopes had outrun their good judgment. His three older brothers, Lawyer, Judge, and Doctor, had actually managed to live up to their peculiar names.

At the very least, Garrison thought his parents could have called him Colonel. Because of their expectations he had enrolled in the Field Artillery Unit of the Army's Reserve Officers' Training Corps, established at the university after the First World War. Garrison had loved the handsome olive-drab breeches and jacket the government provided each ROTC cadet. The only problem was the horses. He hated the beasts.

He eventually resigned his student commission and reluctantly turned in the uniform.

Ah well, Major Garrison sighed to himself. He wrinkled his nose in distaste as he nodded to Siddons, who always seemed to have a smelly, unlit pipe clenched between his stained teeth. From time to time Jim sucked on it, greedily inhaling the last remnants of tobacco-flavored nicotine.

"Come on over, Major," invited Lisle Bradford, the renowned director of East's glee clubs and the elite a cappella choir. She patted the old sofa.

Garrison eyed it with disgust as he took the proffered seat. He primly folded his hands on his lap, careful not to touch the scabrous hide. He winced as a loose spring poked him in the rear, wondering if Miss Bradford had deliberately lured him onto that particular spot.

Her innocent smile betrayed no malice. "We've been discussing that fellow Hitler," she continued.

Garrison snorted. He didn't believe her for a minute. In his opinion, all teachers were indefatigable gossips. He was sure their favorite topics of conversation were the salary scale (too low), the administration (much too preoccupied with pleasing the school board), and—most delicious of all—the personal lives of the East High community. Garrison was positive they talked about *him* behind his back, too.

Before he could raise the topic that had forced him to brave the lounge, the door opened and a tall woman glided into the room.

"Hazel!" A chorus of enthusiastic greetings rose to greet the regal-looking woman as she helped herself to a cup of coffee and tossed a nickel into the chipped mug that served as the faculty's kitty.

"Umm," she murmured with appreciation as she sipped the brew and grinned at her colleagues. "Now that's what I call the 'elixir of life.'"

Garrison couldn't help contrasting her warm reception with his notably cool one. He wondered how Hazel Whitcomb, a new teacher who had initially arrived in the autumn to dark mutterings of 'outsider' and 'taking a job from a breadwinner in these difficult times,' had managed to overcome such obstacles and become accepted so quickly.

"Hazel," Jim rose to her side, "I'd like you to meet Doug Pedersen. He's just been transferred from Granite High to take over the advanced algebra classes. Doug, this is J. Hazel Whitcomb, history teacher extraordinaire."

Hazel extended her hand, giving the newcomer a firm handshake. "I'm pleased to make your acquaintance."

Doug Pedersen's eyebrows rose at her faint British accent.

"Hazel's new herself," Siddons commented. "She's American; married a British diplomat. They lived all over the world. She's got a master's degree in history from Columbia University," he added with obvious pride in his colleague's accomplishments.

"So how did someone with such exalted qualifications end up teaching in our fair city?" Pedersen inquired, curious.

"My husband died last spring," Hazel explained. "Some strange tropical infection the doctors never did figure out. I was at loose ends and didn't know what to do with myself. We didn't have any children. I'd never seen the West, so I came to visit a distant cousin here in Salt Lake City and do a bit of sightseeing. I was also interested in the Mormons—from a historical point of view, of course. I've been impressed by the faith and commitment that drove them to pioneer the Great Basin Area. It isn't the best land for farming, you know. When this job unexpectedly opened, I decided to apply. The rest is, as they say, history.

"I've grown to love this area," Hazel continued as she sat down and made herself comfortable. "The mountains, the desert—I've met wonderful people all over this city. It's much more diverse than I expected. I've been here only a few months but it already feels like home. Derek and I moved so much we never had a real home. I just might stay here forever."

The other faculty members smiled, pleased that such a sophisticated, well-traveled woman would adopt their beloved city.

"Uh, Doug, this is Major Garrison," Siddons inserted, almost as an afterthought. "He's our Dean of Boys."

Garrison dipped his head but kept his hand at his side. He'd noticed Pedersen sniffling and sneezing into a well-used, soggy handkerchief. Garrison had taught biology and boys' health before becoming an administrator. He knew too much about germs to risk infecting himself with a contaminated handshake.

"We had a *very* interesting discussion in our senior U.S. history class this afternoon," Hazel mused. "We're studying the American frontier and the Western expansion during the 1800s. We're examining the Mexican-American War and the concept of 'Manifest Destiny,' to be precise. Once each week we also consider current world events and their implications. I've kept up Derek's mail subscription to the Sunday edition of the *London Times*. It's a couple of weeks old by the time it arrives, but it has a very different perspective from the local papers. I clipped an editorial on Hitler's use of the Enabling Act to establish a one-party dictatorship and read it to the class today."

Hazel continued, "I told the class how Hitler is rousing the people with the Nazi party slogan 'Germany Awake!' He's exhorting the Germans to seize what is rightfully theirs. I'm afraid he considers that to be the rest of Europe. My comments provoked an interesting debate. One of the best students, Tom van Sloten, asked an unusual question. 'Mrs. Whitcomb,' he challenged, 'you've called Japan's invasion of Manchuria two years ago blatant aggression. Now you say the same thing about Hitler's territorial designs on the rest of Europe. Why is that any different from the United States taking Utah, Texas, and California—the whole West, for that matter—from Mexico? I don't see there's much difference between America's so-called Manifest Destiny and the idea of *lebensraum*, or living room, for the German people.'"

"Impertinent!" Major Garrison huffed, offended at the very suggestion that America's acquisitions were anything less than a divinely appointed right.

"I disagree. I thought Tom's question was very perceptive," Hazel rejoined. "The boy's blessed with the curse of an inquiring mind."

Garrison wasn't appeased. "His way of thinking is, well, unpatriotic," he muttered.

"Tom is a very bright, inquisitive young man," Siddons put in. "He was the top student in my algebra class a couple of years ago. Don't know anything about his political persuasions. Or his family's, for that matter. But he does have a rather unusual group of friends."

"Who?"

"Louis Chaffos, for one. He's Greek. Dick Stein. Jewish, of course. And Dean Lindsay. He's half Polynesian."

"*Hah!*" Garrison grunted with a mirthless explosion that was more a bark than a laugh.

Hazel didn't seem surprised at the list of Tom's friends. "Tom doesn't say a lot in class, but when he does, it's quite thought provoking," she continued. "He seems shy, especially around girls. Definitely not part of the student 'in crowd.' He's a rather nice chap, I'd say. Polite. Always neat and tidy, but his clothes are, to put it charitably, a bit on the shabby side."

Phyllis Tregagle, a veteran teacher who was the acknowledged doyenne of the English department, spoke up. "Tom is in my senior English class. Excels in it, too. I also know the van Sloten family. They moved into my neighborhood four, maybe five years ago."

"Ah!" Major Garrison exclaimed. "Then perhaps you'll enlighten us,

Miss Tregagle. How could a bright young man like Tom develop such—shall we say *unusual*—ideas?"

Phyllis Tregagle stiffened at his challenging tone. "I don't know if I can explain what you call Tom's 'unusual ideas.' What I can tell you is that his parents are two of the finest people I've ever known. The family was okay until the Depression hit and Henry lost his job. His health is poor so he isn't suited for manual labor—and that's about the only work anyone can get these days. Henry never complains; quite the opposite, in fact. He and Sarah are always trying to encourage and cheer up everyone else. Henry's a very talented musician. He sings all over the valley—performs at church services, funerals, weddings, concerts. Never charges anyone a dime."

"And the children?"

"Five of them. The older ones all have odd jobs—I think Tom actually has two jobs. He works at Dunford's Bakery before school and at Rosenblatt's Department Store in the afternoon. He's saving for college, but I wonder if he's making much progress. I think he's paid all his own expenses—clothes, books, doctor bills, and the like—since he was ten or twelve years old. Given Henry's difficulties, I suspect Tom's probably helping out with the rest of the family, too."

The basketball coach finally spoke up. "Maybe so, but in my book the kid's a quitter. He tried out for the junior varsity squad last year. Never played basketball before, but he's tall, quick, seemed to have good reflexes. He desperately wanted to be on the team. I decided to take a chance and put him on the squad. I worked him hard, and he seemed to be coming along. Then, without so much as a word of explanation, he quit. It was halfway through the season, too. Far as I'm concerned, van Sloten doesn't have the guts to stick it out when the going gets tough."

"*I* think he has what it takes to succeed," Hazel disagreed. "It would be a real waste if Tom couldn't go to the university. Such a fine mind . . ."

Major Garrison stood up and interrupted the discussion with a far more important topic than the travails of a mere student from an unimportant family. "The money," he remarked, impatient to conclude the business that had brought him to the lounge in the first place.

"Money?" Siddons asked, genuinely puzzled. "What money?"

"*That* money," Garrison said, gesturing at the mug full of loose change.

Lisle Bradford laughed, her ample sides quivering. "Major, 'that money' doesn't amount to much. It's become sort of a standing joke. Times are so tough we claim we'll accept anything, cash or reasonable facsimiles thereof. Hazel contributed a British five-pence piece. I found a New York City bus token in the kitty when I was looking for change. And someone, we're not sure who," she winked at the basketball coach, "actually put in a wooden nickel a couple of days ago!"

Garrison was undeterred. "We—the administration, that is—think it's unwise to have money in *any* amount lying around unaccounted for. These days it's a real temptation. It should be kept in the main office. There should be a detailed, complete record of everything going in and out, too."

Siddons guffawed, incredulous. "So *that's* why you deigned to join our merry band, Garrison!"

Major Garrison colored. "Just *do* it, Siddons! I'm holding you personally responsible," he warned as he stomped out of the lounge and slammed the door.

"That pompous—!" Siddons spat in the direction of Garrison's retreating back.

"He is a little martinet, isn't he?" Hazel Whitcomb agreed.

"Classic example of what happens when someone like that gets a little petty power," Lisle Bradford added.

Phyllis Tregagle nodded, her natural humor dampened. "Garrison gives me the creeps. He reminds me of something—well, not quite human. When I was growing up in Chicago, on Saturdays my parents often took us to places like the Brookfield Zoo or the Science and Industry Museum. Whenever we went to the Shedd Aquarium, my big brothers always insisted on seeing the shark tank. Every single time! They loved it. One day the biggest shark in the tank swam up to the glass and stopped right in front of me. It just hovered there, unblinking, staring at me with those cold, pitiless eyes. Thinking of that reminds me of Major Garrison. He's such a stickler for rules. And when he gets that look in his eyes . . ." Phyllis shivered.

The room fell silent. They all knew exactly what she meant.

❧ CHAPTER FOUR ❧

Early Tuesday afternoon, December 12, 1933

Sarah's natural optimism couldn't overcome the sense of doom that was beginning to engulf the van Sloten family. Even Tom didn't seem his stalwart, normal self these days. Sarah usually hummed as she bent willingly to the unending household chores; today she worked in stolid silence.

Sarah did take some comfort in routines. After all, it just wasn't possible to run a household of seven people crammed into four small rooms without routines. Order and predictability were essential. Growing up in a family of twelve, Sarah had had enough chaos to last a lifetime.

Tuesday—laundry day—was her least favorite day of the week. Monday—baking day—had its intrinsic yeasty compensations. On Wednesdays she and the other neighborhood women met for the Women's Society. She loved the gatherings, not just for the strength the women gained from each other but for the weekly lessons and stimulating discussions.

After Wednesday the week was a long uphill grind until the Sabbath. Thursday was cleaning day. Friday was ironing day. It seemed every day—except for Sunday, of course—was sewing day. Sarah sighed, but just a little. She hated whining.

Saturdays were consumed with Sabbath preparations. Hendrik always set up a chair in the kitchen and gave each of the boys a haircut. He used an old hand clipper with two missing teeth that pulled at the boys' hair. As he was invariably in a hurry, Hendrik would fall into a rapid rhythm of snip and toss as he flipped the hair onto the floor. Once, when he got ahead of himself and started to flip the hair before he clipped it, Tom had winced and joked, "Dad, would you mind cutting the hair before you try to throw it on the floor?"

Every Saturday night Hendrik lit the gas heater in the small bathroom and filled the tub for the family's weekly baths. The standing rule was: The Cleanest Kid Gets to Go in First. The children were motivated to stay as clean as possible.

Sarah pinned another load of laundry to the wire lines in the dining room as they sagged under the weight of the wet clothes. In the chill, the washing often took several days to dry and made the house feel clammy. The family used clean clothes sparingly. Underwear and socks were changed every other day, pants and shirts just once a week. With seven people, the laundry still piled up like a tidal wave.

She took another load into the small utility shed next to the boys' sleeping porch. The tiny room held a small icebox and the family's old but serviceable Maytag washer. She extracted wet clothes from the washer, put them in the rinse tub, and then carefully fed them through the mechanical wringer before she put the next batch in. The process seemed unending.

As she reentered the house with a fresh bunch of laundry, Sarah heard footsteps outside the house followed by a metallic clang. She peered outside. It was the postman, putting the van Slotens' mail in the rusted box on the front porch.

Sarah waited until he clumped off the porch and was well out of sight before she retrieved the mail. She was sure he knew that most of the envelopes contained unpaid bills. As she sorted through the letters, she was relieved to see they weren't all bills. There were actually even a few Christmas cards. The van Slotens didn't send cards themselves, so they received only a few from their most loyal, better-off friends.

At long last all the laundry was washed and hung out to dry. Sarah collapsed on the sofa, too tired to do anything but close her eyes for a few blessed minutes. Thankfully, her sister-in-law had taken the younger boys for the day. The house was quiet, the stillness interrupted only by the monotonous, rhythmic ticking of the old grandfather clock Henry's father had brought from the Netherlands.

She drifted into a light, dreamless sleep. The unexpected sound of heavy, shuffling footsteps on the porch startled her into instant wakefulness. The mail had already come. She glanced at the clock. It was still too early for the older children to be home from school.

The door creaked open and Hendrik stumbled into the room, ashen with fatigue. Sarah jumped up and hugged her husband, suddenly conscious of how thin he had become. He sagged against her, his dead weight making her stagger. She helped him to the sofa, easing him onto the lumpy cushions. Sarah sat down beside him, pulling off his worn cloth cap. She cradled his head on her shoulder and stroked his hair.

They sat in silence for a moment. Finally, taking her husband's work-roughened hands, Sarah asked slowly, "Henry . . . ?"

He refused to meet her worried eyes, shaking his head in mute despair.

"Nothing," he finally said. "There was nothing at all today. At least not for me. No one wants a weak old man who can barely lift a shovel without gasping for breath."

Sarah tried to appear unconcerned. "Maybe tomorrow—"

Hendrik shook his head, cutting her off. "Tomorrow won't be any different. Sarah, I can't—"

"Shhh," she hushed, gently putting a finger to his thin lips, noticing they still looked blue from the cold. "We'll think of something."

Hendrik leaned forward, twisting his hands until they were white. "Sarah, it's worse. I have a confession to make. I did something I shouldn't have. I haven't been honest with you."

Sarah caught her breath, bile rising in her throat. Every woman's fear . . . but certainly not Hendrik! He was the *last* one who would ever . . . He would rather be stretched on the rack than violate his marriage vows. Surely not . . .

Hendrik stared at the floor, unable to look at his wife. "Last night, when I gave you the money I made working on the water line . . . well, I didn't give it all to you. I kept some back. I was *so* tired. Exhausted. Sarah, I didn't think I could walk all the way home tonight. So I put a nickel in my pocket for the streetcar. I shouldn't have done it, I know. We just can't afford it."

Sarah didn't know whether to laugh or cry. So she did both. "Oh, Henry," she choked, starting to reassure him.

"No," he interrupted her again. "Something worse happened, Sarah. *Far* worse. I disgraced the church."

Sarah was stunned. It was the last thing in the world she would have believed. Henry's faith was rock solid, his commitment unquestioned. Or so she had always thought. Their love for each other and shared beliefs were the bedrock of their relationship, constants in a rising sea of uncertainty.

"I should never had gotten on that darned streetcar," he repeated as he hung his head. "You know that place where our line intersects the one that comes down from the university?"

Sarah nodded, not knowing what was coming next.

"I was sitting way in the back when the conductor opened the door. Rolf Jacobsen and Ted Gaines got on," Henry said, referring to two high-level officials with whom he served in the church. "They must have been up there for a meeting. They're on some sort of committee for the university. Both of them were in business suits with white shirts and ties. Carrying briefcases and wearing fedoras, too. I pulled my cap real low and slumped as far down in the seat as I could, hoping they wouldn't recognize me. Not in these," Hendrik pointed with embarrassment at his threadbare work clothes and dirty boots.

"But of course, they did," he continued. "They came all the way to the back, shook my hand, and sat down right beside me. Acted like they were real pleased to see me, too. They started in talking about church issues. Neither of them ever said a word about how I looked. And how badly I reflect on the church, dressed like this."

Sarah took Hendrik's gnarled hands and squeezed them gently. "Henry, just remember: The scriptures say man looks on the outward appearance, but the Lord looks on the heart. He knows *your* heart, Henry. And so do I."

Hendrik touched her cheek. Then he leaned back on the worn sofa and closed his eyes. Sarah remained beside him in the waning afternoon, keeping a silent vigil.

❧ CHAPTER FIVE ☙

Later Tuesday afternoon, December 12, 1933

O ne down, one to go. Tom fingered the sealed Utah Power and Light envelope. It felt thin, much too light to hold the full payment. He suspected this time his mother had included barely enough to keep UP&L from shutting off their electricity. She always insisted he stand in line at the window and get a written receipt. Tom hated it when the amount fell short of what was due. Maybe it was only his imagination, but the clerk— annoyingly smug in his own secure job with the utility company—would record the amount and then shoot him a disdainful look.

This time Tom dropped the envelope through the slot marked Payments Due and left without a receipt. He simply couldn't endure another encounter with the supercilious man.

He walked from the UP&L office past the Daynes Jewelry Building on South Main. The late afternoon sky, almost obscured by the patchwork of wires and cables that arched over the streetcar tracks, was darkened by soft coal smoke belching from innumerable chimneys. His mood matched the gloom. The city had put up a few scrawny wreaths on the electric street-lights. They seemed forlorn, painful reminders of a long-gone prosperity.

The local merchants had decorated their windows in bright red and green, displaying merchandise that few in the Depression-strapped city could afford. Even the Salt Lake 5 & 10 Cent Store was mostly empty of customers. Tom looked at the shiny toys in its windows and sighed.

He rounded the corner and pushed through the back entrance to Rosenblatt's Department Store. At twenty-five cents an hour, the pay was good. But when people weren't buying and there were few items to replace, he felt lucky to have even the few hours a week his part-time job as a stock boy provided.

"Hey, Tom!" his supervisor greeted him affably. "You're early. Get kicked out of school or sumpin'?" He chuckled.

Tom shook his head, too depressed to join in the customary banter.

"We got even less to do than usual," the older man reported. "Business ain't too good. Guess the big Christmas shopping boost isn't goin' tuh happen this year. Old Man Rosenblatt must be gettin' a mite worried, what with all this expensive stuff that nobody's buyin'. I'm gonna have tuh send ya home an hour early today. Real sorry, kid, but there's nothin' I can do." He spread his hands in an apologetic shrug.

Tom, resigned to losing the much-needed extra pay, didn't bother to respond.

"Say!" the supervisor remarked, suddenly remembering. "Do you have a sister? Real pretty gal, sorta looks like you? Dark hair, fair complected?"

Tom nodded.

"Hmm. Coulda sworn I saw her in the store today. She was lookin' at fancy party dresses."

Tom laughed aloud at the absurd thought. "I don't think so," he said. "It must have been somebody else. Jeannie baby-sits after school. Besides which, she'd never shop here anyway."

The supervisor looked dubious. He thought a moment, then rubbed his chin and nodded, "Yeah. You're prob'ly right. Couldn' ta been your sister after all. Awful pretty, though."

Their few tasks completed all too quickly, Tom left the storeroom and trudged down Main Street. He passed the 5 & 10, too discouraged to stop and admire the appealing display. For a fleeting moment he considered . . . no. He put the unbidden thought firmly out of his mind. He *had* to keep his priorities straight. It would take everything he had already saved plus a summer of hard work to accumulate enough for his fall quarter tuition and fees at the university.

The farther he walked toward home, the more unsettled he felt. On an impulse, he detoured into Liberty Park. Its tall, barren trees looked like skeletons with uplifted arms, beseeching the gunmetal sky. A light wind rustled in the branches, scratching a mournful tune that made him shudder. To save money, the city had shut off almost all the lights within the park itself. The dark both beckoned and repelled him.

Overcoming his fear, Tom waded through the dirty snow piled along the pathways that wound through the park until he found a quiet, undisturbed spot. He sank to his knees and, heedless of the cold, cried out for help and reassurance. He prayed for relief from the depression that seemed ready to overwhelm him. He pleaded for his struggling family. He asked for the courage and determination to stick to his goals.

The heavens remained silent, closed to his entreaties.

Tom's shoulders sagged. He finally rose, dark blotches on his knees where the wet had seeped through the thin pants.

He would never know exactly when it happened. But between the park and home, it came to him. He didn't hear a voice or even a whisper. It was more like a gentle but insistent thought. *He,* Tom, could be Santa! It would consume his college savings, but if he had a shot at the new history scholarship . . . His feelings of doubt and confusion lightened as he felt a quiet peace drop over him like a heaven-sent shield.

Full of gratitude, he crept in the back door of his house to the sleeping porch and opened his dresser drawer. He emptied the glass jar onto the bed and counted. Sixteen dollars and twenty-three cents. Would it be enough? A meticulous planner, he opened his school notebook to a clean page and began composing a list. What made up a Christmas celebration, anyway?

First, the tree, he thought. Some people got permits and cut one for free in the Wasatch National Forest east of the city. Without a car, that was out of the question. He would have to purchase one from a commercial lot. *How much is a tree?* He'd never bought one. He needed to do a bit of research.

He stepped outside and retrieved the morning newspaper from a neighbor's trash. Finding the advertising section, he hastily scanned the columns. "Montana Fir Christmas trees are the best by extreme test," one ad boasted. Another cried, "Guaranteed not to shed needles! Very bushy and symmetrical. The finest trees at any price for any home. Sizes 3 to 18 feet available. Prices Below Average."

What does "Prices Below Average" mean? he wondered.

On another page, a prominent ad from the downtown Grand Central department store was touting the "largest selection in the city. Priced low for quick sell," it enticed. That wasn't very informative, either.

Tom finally found an inconspicuous notice with a single sentence that stated, "Montana Fir Christmas trees guaranteed not to shed their needles, twenty-five cents and up." That was more like it! Even better, the lot was within walking distance.

He licked his pencil tip and wrote:

Christmas tree $ .25

Next, decorations. The strings of fat colored lights they all loved were stored in the unfinished basement along with the family ornament collection. In addition, there were several boxes of the fragile silver icicles his father placed strand by delicate strand on the tree. They were always painstakingly removed after the holidays and kept for use again the following year. That would have to do. No new ornaments this year.

Lights. It reminded him of the overdue bills stacked on the kitchen counter. It wouldn't be much of a holiday in a cold, dark house. Worse, if they were evicted, they'd have no house at all. That meant coal, water, probably more money for UP&L. Rent, too. He wouldn't have to pay the whole thing, of course. These days, almost no one did. All he needed to do was set aside just enough to keep the creditors satisfied for another month. How much would be enough?

He guessed and wrote:

Christmas tree $ .25
Utilities, rent, etc. $9.00

Tom gulped. More than half the budget was already gone.

Dinner. The family usually spent about five dollars a week for food. But what about a once-in-a-year, special celebration? He had no idea how much a turkey cost. Chicken, a special Sunday treat, was twelve cents a pound. What about everything else that went with a Christmas dinner? Dressing, sweet potatoes, peas, cranberry sauce, pies, the usual stuff. He'd have to estimate.

Christmas tree $ .25
Utilities, rent, etc. $9.00
Dinner $3.00

He groaned. At the beginning, sixteen dollars had seemed like a small fortune. Tom was appalled at how rapidly the expenses mounted. And he hadn't even started on the presents yet! No wonder his father worried all the time! He winced, remembering how critical he'd felt about his father's constant preoccupation with money. It seemed so demeaning. Now he understood why Hendrik fretted so much.

Presents, he wrote next. Now he was in more familiar territory. He had purchased toys for the younger children before.

Christmas tree	$ .25
Utilities, rent, etc.	$9.00
Dinner	$3.00
Presents	$3.00
Jean	
Richard	
Paul	
David	

Three dollars wasn't much, but it would have to do unless he could find a third part-time job. That was unlikely in such desperate times. He longed to give his parents a modest gift as well, but it just didn't seem feasible.

Contingencies. The so-called financial experts urged people to plan for emergencies. They recommended a minimum of 10 percent of one's budget. He laughed wryly, trying to avoid feeling bitter. In the van Sloten family, *every* day was a financial emergency. He didn't have 10 percent. Not even close! But he would allocate the last few cents for the unexpected.

Christmas tree	$ .25
Utilities, rent, etc.	$9.00

Dinner	$3.00
Presents	$3.00
Jean	
Richard	
Paul	
David	
Contingencies	$ .98

That was it. He had budgeted every last penny. *I can actually do this,* he thought. It would be close, but he could pull it off. Maybe. It depended on how well he could do with the presents. He briefly considered taking Jean into his confidence, asking her to contribute some of her baby-sitting funds. Then he discarded the idea. Jeannie hoarded her money. Even if he could talk her into parting with some of her hard-earned cash, she was such a show-off she'd probably blab about it and ruin the whole thing. *Forget about Jeannie,* he decided.

Tom closed his notebook, put the money back in the jar, and returned it to its hiding place. Now the real challenge was to persuade his parents. Above all, he wanted to preserve what remained of his father's shredded dignity. That meant his role would have to remain anonymous.

He would need to be a secret Santa.

"Dinner's ready!" Tom heard his mother summon the family. He hurried to his accustomed spot on the bench. Davey offered the prayer, his high voice squeaking out the "thank yous" and "please blesses" with enthusiasm. Tom could almost hear the smiles in the amens that followed.

"Treats two nights in a row!" his mother announced a bit too brightly as she carried the platter of chocolate doughnuts to the table. "A dozen Dunford doughnuts and ice-cold milk to top it off!"

She put two doughnuts on Hendrik's plate, then two more on each of the four older children's plates. She kept one apiece for herself and Davey. Tom saw his little brother's face fall. Without hesitating, he picked up one of his own doughnuts and divided it in half, giving the larger piece to Davey.

"Let's share, Davey! Besides, I already ate one this morning," he lied. He felt a twinge of guilt at the untruth, telling himself it was in a good cause.

Davey grinned as he wolfed down the doughnut, smearing chocolate icing all over his face. He smacked his lips as he licked each finger clean.

No one commented about the odd meal.

Jean and Tom carried the dirty dishes into the kitchen. Tom lifted the heavy cast-iron pot of water that had been heating on the coal stove. Steam billowed up from the pot as he poured the water into a chipped enamel dishpan in the sink. Before he had even set the pot down, Jean had grabbed the dish towel. "It's your turn to wash," she said. "I'll dry."

"Jeannie, I washed last night. It's *your* turn," Tom protested. They both hated washing. The harsh Fels Naptha soap chapped their hands and left a strong, unpleasant chemical odor that clung to the skin for hours.

"No it isn't," Jean retorted. "You always say that."

"It is too your turn! You have a convenient memory, Jeannie. *I* washed last night. You dried," he bickered.

"Didn't either! *I* washed, *you* dried!"

"*Jeannie!*" Fed up, Tom grabbed his sister's arm roughly just as Sarah entered the kitchen.

"Tom!" she scolded. "You know better than that. You wash, Jeannie will dry."

Seething at the injustice, Tom grabbed the bar of soap and began whittling small chunks into the steaming hot dishwater. The shavings slowly dissolved, leaving a scummy film in the pan. He plunged his hands into the scalding brown water, trying to ignore the smell as he scrubbed, rinsed, and handed the wet dishes to Jeannie. She smiled, all injured innocence.

Tom fumed in silence.

Trying to ignore his anger, Tom waited until the other children had finished their homework and gone to bed. Then he drew his parents into the dining room and closed the door. A wet shirt brushed his cheek and twanged the wires as he ducked under the damp wash.

"Mom, Dad," he began his carefully rehearsed presentation as he faced his parents. "I've been thinking about Christmas. I've got an idea or two that just might work."

Hendrik folded his arms across his chest.

"Dad, *I* could be Santa Claus," Tom rushed on. "Get the kids' presents. I can do the whole thing myself. I've saved enough money . . ." Tom paused as Hendrik's mouth set in a hard line. He shook his head in flat refusal.

Tom tried another approach. "Well then, how about considering the whole thing as an interest-free loan?"

"No. Absolutely not!" Hendrik grunted.

"Dad, please hear me out. Don't be a stubborn Dutch—" Tom began.

"Don't say that! *Ever!*" his father flared.

"Henry!" Sarah cried, startled at her husband's uncharacteristic display of temper.

"I'm not just being stubborn," Hendrik protested, unaccustomed heat in his voice. "Tom's worked hard for that money. He needs it for college. Every bit of it. *Somebody* in this poor family has got to break the pattern. For generations the van Slotens have been nothing more than crofters—peasants, really—and day laborers. Education is the key, at least it is here in America. Any fool can see that as plain as day!"

"But Dad, I really *want* to do this," Tom persisted. "Would you deny me the blessing of being the Santa this year? Just this once? The university can wait a year," he added, hoping it wouldn't be longer.

Sarah glanced at her husband. She knew that accepting Tom's well-meaning generosity would exacerbate Hendrik's feelings of inadequacy. But what were the alternatives? With tears in her eyes, she nodded an almost imperceptible *yes*.

Hendrik overruled her. "No, Tom, I can't let you be Santa. That's *my* job."

"But Dad—"

"*No!* I said no. And that's final!" Hendrik growled as he stormed out of the dining room.

Tom looked at his mother in mute appeal. Sarah shrugged and shook her head. Hendrik had decided. The matter was closed.

❦ CHAPTER SIX ❦

Tuesday night, December 12, 1933

Deflated, Tom stood alone in the darkened dining room, surrounded by damp laundry and the wreckage of his Christmas plans. The feeling in the park had been so strong he couldn't ignore it. But what could he do? His father's emphatic "*No!*" still rang in his ears. He walked into the living room and stared at the barren spot in front of the window, trying to rub the fatigue out of his eyes. Then his face lit up. Surely his father wouldn't begrudge him one small act of anonymous generosity. A tree. A tree for the family to decorate and enjoy and celebrate in song.

It was the least he could do. And maybe, if he did get a tree, the Christmas mood it brought into the house would be enough to change Hendrik's mind about the rest of the plan.

Tom tiptoed onto the sleeping porch, trying not to wake the younger boys. He slid his drawer open and extracted four quarters from the jar. A look of fierce determination on his face, he slipped out the back door and sprinted the six blocks to the nearest Christmas tree lot. The lot stood on a busy corner, outlined by strings of bare lightbulbs. The place was redolent of fresh pine and sawn wood. He was the only customer.

The proprietor, bundled in a thick muffler and stamping his feet to stay warm, stood near a fire he had kindled in a rusted oil drum. "Can I help you?" he chirped.

"I need a large, fat tree. Well-formed. Symmetric," Tom answered, out of breath but pleased with himself for sounding so knowledgeable.

"What kind? Scotch pine? White pine? Doug fir?"

Tom's confidence evaporated. "Uh, well, the exact kind doesn't matter. Appearance does. How 'bout that one?" he queried, pointing to a handsome specimen.

"Well, you've got a fine eye for trees," the owner flattered his young customer. "And that one's a real bargain. It's marked down from eighty-nine to seventy-nine cents. Special for you, I'll throw in a wreath for nothing!"

Suddenly deflated, Tom countered, "On second thought, that one may be a bit too big for our usual spot. Do you have something smaller?"

The owner beckoned to a row of shorter but nicely shaped trees. "These six-footers are sixty-nine cents. The five-foot ones go for fifty-nine. And the spruce trees in the next row are all forty-nine each."

Tom's shoulders sagged. He was already over budget and he had barely started. "Maybe I'll just walk around a bit and look for a while," he temporized.

"Suit yourself." The owner shrugged and walked back to the welcoming fire. "If you find anything you want, just holler!"

Tom strolled up and down each aisle, looking hard. There wasn't a row of twenty-five-cent trees. He felt defeated. As he finished scanning the lot, he noticed a scraggly tree in the corner leaning against a light post. He examined it. No tag anywhere.

"Hey!" he shouted. "What about this one right here?"

"Aw, you don't want that one," the proprietor protested, trying to turn

Tom back toward the more expensive trees. "That's a subalpine fir. A trash tree. A few of them got in the last load by mistake. I've been cutting them up to make wreaths."

Tom didn't move. He stared at the misshapen tree. "How much?" he persisted.

The owner gave in. "I'll let you have it for twenty cents."

Tom tried to convince himself that the scrawny tree wasn't as ugly as it looked. "Okay," he decided, encouraged that he would now be *under* budget. "Can I have some of those sawed-off branches over there?" he added with an innocent look.

The proprietor looked at the pile of branches, then peered over his spectacles at Tom. His eyes softened. "Son, you know how to do what I think you're gonna do?" he asked gently.

"I guess so. Maybe."

The proprietor shot his customer a dubious glance. "You know, I got nothin' else better to do tonight. Might as well do some useful work. Here! Let an old tree dog show ya a few tricks of the trade!" Without waiting for a reply, he grasped Tom's tree and carried it to his workbench. He picked up a hand drill and bored a series of slanted holes in its trunk. Then, searching through the pile of discarded branches, he selected a few choice limbs and expertly whittled their ends to fit the holes. He finished by inserting the branches into the trunk and gluing them securely into place.

The proprietor stood back and admired his work.

The tree was transformed.

"It looks . . . wonderful!" Tom breathed, hardly daring to ask. "Now how much?"

The proprietor pretended astonishment. "Why, twenty cents! That's what I said, didn't I? Everybody in this-here city knows old Jack Price is a man of his word!"

"You sure are," Tom agreed as he produced a quarter. Pocketing the change, he hefted the tree over his shoulder.

Christmas had started with a minor miracle.

Whistling happily under his breath, Tom crept up the steps with his treasure and stopped on the porch, listening for a moment. The house was dark, the quiet punctuated only by Jean's soft snores. He wrestled the tree through the front door, taking care not to dislodge any of its newly implanted branches. He positioned the tree in front of the living-room window.

Then he smiled, relishing the thought of the family's surprise in the morning.

❧ CHAPTER SEVEN ❧
Wednesday morning, December 13, 1933

J ean huddled under her blanket, aware that something had changed during the night. The house, still dark in the predawn chill, was subtly different. Then she had it. The van Sloten home smelled of pine, the unmistakable scent of Christmas. Yawning, she stretched as Hendrik came into the living room in his worn bathrobe and slippers. He cracked the smoldering coal open and stirred up the fire. In the sudden blaze, they both spied the tree that had magically appeared during the night.

"Sarah!" Hendrik roared.

She stumbled out of their bedroom, eyes crinkling with surprise. Roused by their father's shout, the children poured into the living room. Before Hendrik could say another word, the younger boys started jumping with excitement, skipping and dancing around the tree in their joy.

"A tree! A *tree!*" Paul squealed in delight.

"It's Christmas! It's really Christmas!" Richard chanted as they circled the undecorated tree.

Tom held his breath, awaiting his father's judgment. Would the family's obvious delight temper his displeasure at having been disobeyed? Would Hendrik's experienced gaze detect the cosmetic surgery?

Frowning, Hendrik walked around the tree, examining it from every angle. He pursed his lips. At last he proclaimed, "It's a splendid Christmas tree." A broad grin split his tired face. "We'll decorate it tonight!"

"Whoopee!" the little boys shouted. "Tonight! We decorate the tree *tonight!*"

Tom exhaled in relief.

"Let's get it in water right away," Hendrik said. He took a small handsaw from his toolbox and removed the bottom inch of its trunk while Tom fetched the tree stand from the basement. Together they clamped the tree securely in place and filled the well to its top. Then Hendrik took Tom by the arm, firmly steering him toward the bedroom. "The three of us need to have a little chat, son. You, your mother, and I."

Hendrik closed the door gently. Before he could say a word, Tom blurted, "Dad, I just wanted to—"

"I told you no, Tom. And I meant it. You disobeyed."

"Tom means well, Henry," Sarah interceded. "I know it's hard to let him do what we can't. But the children—" She stopped at the hurt on Hendrik's face. He groaned as a tear squeezed out and trickled down his cheek.

"Henry," Sarah pleaded.

"The kids won't know," Tom added, sensing his father's resolve weakening. "It'll just be between us."

Hendrik sighed with reluctance.

"Please, Dad. I can't tell you how much it would mean to me. *Please* let me be Santa Claus. Just this once!" Tom pleaded.

"All right, son," Hendrik relented. "But only if you let us tell the children. I say give credit where credit's due."

Tom shook his head. "Then the deal's off," he replied firmly. "Secret or no Santa!"

Conflicting emotions swept across Hendrik's drawn face. Then he slapped his knee and laughed out loud, partly in relief but mostly out of respect for his son's fierce determination. "Okay," he agreed. "You're relentless, son. But there's one condition."

Tom waited as his father explained. "As I've told you before, I was only seven when my parents brought us to Utah. They were in the great wave of immigrants that left Scotland and Ireland in the early part of this century. They ended up in Magna, where your granddad got a job in the copper mines. He thought education beyond the eighth grade—which the law required—was foolishness. He insisted I go to work and help support the family. If I lived at home, that would include paying room and board once I finished school.

"You know that part. What I never told you is we had a terrible argument. Tom, Granddad really *was* a 'stubborn Dutchman.' He absolutely refused to see the necessity of changing the old ways. We ended up yelling at each other. He got so red in the face I thought he was going to have an apoplectic fit right on the spot. I ran out of the house and swore I'd never go back. And I didn't, not for two long years." Hendrik shut his eyes at the painful memory. "I was only fourteen, but I moved into a boardinghouse in Salt Lake City so I could go to West High School. I worked nights as an usher at the old Salt Lake Theatre and cleaned the boardinghouse toilets in exchange for my room and board."

Hendrik sighed with regret. "Your mother and I aren't in a position to help with your tuition and fees at the university. Chances are we never will be, either. But we want to do our part. Tom, what we *can* do is allow you to live at home without paying room and board until you finish your degree."

Tom's eyes stung. It was an extraordinary offer. He had known he was expected to pay for his own support once he finished high school. He had never imagined anything else. He'd been contributing to the family finances since he was ten and had taken real pride in pulling more than his share of the load. He started to protest, then stopped at the hurt look in his father's eyes. "Fair enough," Tom conceded, suddenly understanding the symbolic importance of accepting his father's offer. "That'll be a huge help, Dad. I can't thank you enough. It'll make a big difference—just maybe *the* difference."

Hendrik straightened, satisfied. "Deal?" he insisted, sticking out his hand.

"Deal!" Tom shook it and gave his father a big hug.

Santa was in business.

☙ CHAPTER EIGHT ❧

Wednesday night, December 13, 1933

Under Hendrik's exacting direction, trimming the tree required an entire evening. The anticipation was delicious as the family rushed through dinner, hardly noticing the spartan meal. Jean washed the dishes without a word of complaint as Tom cleaned up the kitchen.

Boxes of ornaments littered the living-room floor. Hendrik rearranged them in a strictly predetermined order, then began the ritual by positioning fat colored electric bulbs around the tree. He started with a white one at the very top and then wound the strings lower and lower until he reached the bottom of the tree. He replaced a few burned-out lights as he went, clipping each securely in place. Then he plugged the strands together.

"Ooooh!" the children exclaimed in unison as color danced around the room.

Hendrik stepped back, eyeing the tree. He repositioned a few bulbs, moving each one to correct what he called "dark spots." After several attempts, he achieved the requisite balance and symmetry.

Ropes of much-used tinsel and strands of red and green construction paper glued into chains with flour paste came next, followed by strings of cranberries and fresh popcorn. Sarah emptied the boxes, giving each child a shiny ornament. Holding them in both hands, the children carried the fragile ornaments to Hendrik. The small ones went on top, the larger ones were placed in the middle, and the giant glass balls were hung on the largest branches at the bottom of the tree. Hendrik strategically positioned each ornament next to a light.

Sarah had spent the morning making gingerbread boys and sugar cookies for the children to tie on the tree. They worked eagerly, "accidentally" breaking several cookies and eagerly consuming them along the way.

The next step was the most critical part of the process, one that Hendrik reserved for himself. The children watched in awe. He reached into the last box and pulled out the fragile silver icicles that were removed each year and painstakingly wound around cardboard holders for safekeeping. Hendrik draped them one by one over each branch until the tree shimmered in glory.

"This year Tom will place the star," Hendrik announced, relinquishing his traditional prerogative. Climbing the ladder to the very top, Tom solemnly took the glittering star from his father. He pushed the white bulb through its center and fastened it to the highest branch.

Sarah switched off the living-room lights.

The tree was a glorious sight. The family filed outside to admire their handiwork from the sidewalk. Hendrik started to sing in a fine baritone as everyone chorused with "O Tannenbaum."

Christmas had arrived.

Tom hung back as the family trooped back inside. "Jeannie," he whispered to his sister. "We need to talk."

"*Here?* Right on the sidewalk? It's *cold*, Thomas van Sloten, just in case you hadn't noticed!" she protested.

"Here. Now."

Jeannie tucked her bare hands inside the sleeves of her sweater. "Make it quick," she snapped.

"Jeannie, were you in Rosenblatt's yesterday?"

A startled look crossed her face. "No, I wasn't," she said with studied casualness.

"Are you sure?"

Her eyes fell, sliding away from Tom's glare. He waited.

"So what if I was? It's none of your business!" she exploded.

"My supervisor in the stockroom says he saw you in the store looking at clothes. Fancy party dresses," Tom accused.

Jean shrugged.

"Jeannie, I know what those clothes cost. One dress would feed this family for a whole month!"

"Well, Mr. Know-It-All, I haven't bought anything! Not a single thing!"

"But you're *thinking* about it!"

"It's *my* money," Jean flared. "I earned it. Every nickel of it! Taking care of screaming babies with smelly diapers and snot running out of their noses!"

Her defiance rocked Tom. "How—how can you even think about spending that kind of money when our family hardly has enough to eat? Chocolate doughnuts for dinner, for heaven's sake!"

Jeannie gritted her teeth. "I'll tell you just exactly *how* I can think like that. Tom, do you want to live like *this* for the rest of your life?" She gestured at their shabby home in disgust.

Tom was too stunned to answer.

"Well, I don't! Not *this* girl. Nosiree! I'm getting out any way I can! And 'out' means some rich boy from Federal Heights. There are tons of parties up there over the holidays. You can't imagine what they're like. Those people don't even know what the word *Depression* means!"

Jeannie stepped close to Tom, their frozen breaths dueling in the icy air. She poked him in the chest. "And *I* plan to be there! Me! Jean van Sloten. In a dress that will make me look like a million bucks! With expensive perfume and my hair all done up in a chic twist like this!" She piled her hair on the top of her head and then let it slowly fall as she gave her brother a pouty, sultry look.

Tom shook his head in dismay. "Oh, Jeannie . . ."

She was unfazed. "You have your ways. And I have mine." Turning, she stomped up the steps, slamming the front door behind her.

Tom stood rooted to the sidewalk, staring at the tree.

Somehow its lights didn't seem quite as bright.

CHAPTER NINE

Thursday, December 14, 1933

Jean was furious. Just thinking about her heated exchange with Tom the night before made her mad all over again. The week had started well enough. The center on East High's basketball team had asked her for a date, even though she was only a sophomore. Unlike the other guys, he had approached her directly. She liked that. It was nauseating the way some boys tried to ingratiate themselves with Tom, thinking he would "fix them up" with her. As far as social skills went, Tom was hopeless. Why, he didn't even recognize it when girls tried to let him know they liked him! On the rare occasions when it was so obvious even a total dummy couldn't miss it, he would just blush and stammer.

The "Big Date" was for the Sock Hop after tonight's basketball game with arch-rival West High. Jean was sitting in English class, daydreaming about what she would wear and rehearsing the clever things she could say that would impress a senior man with her wit and sophistication.

"Jean!" Mrs. Bates reproved, stunning her back to reality. "I *asked* you to read Robert Frost's poem to the class and tell us what you think he means by the road 'less traveled by.' Don't make me ask a third time!"

Jean hastily thumbed through the textbook, searching in vain for the passage. She hadn't read the assignment last night; she'd been too tired. Besides, Mrs. Bates hardly ever called on her anyway.

"I, uh . . ."

"I thought so," Mrs. Bates interrupted, sniffing with disapproval. "We'll continue the discussion tomorrow. We'll spend the rest of our time today reviewing the poetry homework assignment."

Mrs. Bates waddled down the aisle, handing back the marked papers. She dropped Jean's handwritten sheet on her desk. Jean glanced at it and suppressed a gasp. There were no comments. No grade. Nothing.

"See me after school," Mrs. Bates commanded.

A little knot of fear congealed in Jean's stomach. Mrs. Bates was her least favorite teacher. She was a stern, plain woman who cared deeply about language and literature and seemed interested in little else. She was immune to Jean's charm and had awarded her an unbroken string of C's—and one ignoble D—since the beginning of school. Jean loathed the old battle-ax.

Jean ground her teeth in frustration. To make matters worse, she had a lucrative baby-sitting job lined up for the afternoon. She had big plans for that money, too. She had been saving for weeks for a New Year's Eve party in the exclusive Federal Heights neighborhood. Of course the invitation didn't specifically say so, but the occasion mandated a new outfit. She had seen the perfect dress at Rosenblatt's, a rich velvet sheath that would empha-size her shapely figure. Now she'd have to get a substitute sitter. And pay *her* the bonus she'd been counting on.

Jean sighed. She didn't dare disobey Mrs. Bates.

After school, Jean procrastinated as long as she could. Then she trudged up the three flights of stairs to Mrs. Bates's classroom, dread dogging every step. Mrs. Bates was at her desk, absorbed in a book Jean didn't recognize.

She stood in the doorway, leaning insolently against the frame. Mrs. Bates ignored her. *I'll be darned if I'm going to say something!* Jean fumed inwardly, resenting the whole occasion.

Mrs. Bates finally closed her book and glanced up, a pensive look on her face. "Ah, Jean! Come in. Sit," she said, pointing at a chair next to her desk.

Jean sat.

"Your last homework assignment. The Christmas poem I asked everyone to compose. You have it with you, I presume?" Mrs. Bates had an annoying way of making every question into a statement.

Jean nodded, radiating defiance.

"Read it to me," Mrs. Bates ordered.

"Out loud?" Jean asked, perplexed.

"Of course 'out loud.' Begin with the title."

"I really don't want to," Jean demurred, suddenly shy.

Mrs. Bates fixed her with a look that brooked no argument.

"It's titled 'Christmas Eve, 1929.' So it's not about *this* Christmas," Jean cautioned.

Mrs. Bates waited.

Jean took a deep breath and held up the paper, surprised that her hand was trembling.

> *Ear ache paralyzed*
> *The sluggish hours.*
> *Neither Mother's songs*

Nor my loved quilt of sunbonnet girls
Nor even eggnog
In Grandmother's ruby glass
Could give relief.

Through weeping windowpanes
I watched a million snowflakes
Layer us in endless comforters.
At last, night spread a coverlet,
And creaky gate announced
Our dad was home.

Soon my brothers nested
On the floor, transfixed
As Daddy worked his annual magic
With a fragrant pine.
But on my couch of restlessness
A fevered haze surrounded me;
My tears gave every colored light
A Star-of-David shape,
And tinsel-shine became
A part of pain.

Jean paused, flinching with remembered agony. She glanced up and was startled to see Mrs. Bates's eyes brim with tears.

"Continue," Mrs. Bates ordered in a voice roughened with emotion.

It seemed I dreamed
That distant sleighbells
Tossed their gifts of gladness

Through the quiet night,
But soon the joyful jingling
Arrived at our back door
And portly Mr. Peterson
Squeezed himself with bulging pack
Inside the room.

Repeatedly our old friend's
Dappled, palsied hand
Disappeared within the pack
And found a home-wrapped gift
For each of us.
Doll dishes for me!
Blue glass dishes of my very own!

Then he stooped to gather up the wilted pack
And murmured that he really could not stay,
Then quickly turned to leave.
But we all saw wet wrinkles
Line his cheeks and teardrops
Caught on tips of his moustache.

Then he was gone,
Shuffling a path
Back to his empty, silent house.
The bells were still.
But new pain rang in me.

A minute or two passed, the classroom silence broken only by ticks from the big wall clock.

Mrs. Bates looked at Jean, empathy softening her stern features. "Jean, you surprised me. Perhaps I should have guessed that you have a poet's soul. You hide it very well."

Jean shrugged, at a loss for words.

"With some work you could be good. *Very* good, I should think," Mrs. Bates mused as she reached for Jean's paper and marked the top with a large A.

Jean flushed at the unaccustomed praise. "Don't tell anyone, *please!*" she begged.

Mrs. Bates threw her head back and laughed in genuine amusement. "I won't ruin your image!" she promised. "You've spent a great deal of time and effort cultivating it." Then she grew serious. "One word of caution. A rebel and a romantic. That's a potent combination. A highly combustible one, in fact. Use it. Feed on it. But don't let it consume you. It can, you know."

Jean grinned, realizing her once-despised teacher knew her far better than she could have possibly imagined.

"A last question," Mrs. Bates added. "The assignment was to write a poem anticipating *this* Christmas, about your feelings *now*, not remembering a past Christmas. You didn't do that. Why?"

Jean hung her head, hating to admit the truth. "Santa—I mean Mr. Peterson—died last year. Dad's been out of work for more than two years. I don't think we'll have Christmas this year, Mrs. Bates. Not unless a miracle happens."

❧ CHAPTER TEN ❧

Friday afternoon, December 15, 1933

The American History class quieted as Hazel Whitcomb pulled down a map that depicted the United States in the mid-1850s. She cleared her throat. "Who can tell me what the major differences between a map of the USA that had been drawn in 1848 and this one would . . ."

A hand shot up before she could complete her question. "Yes, Eliza?" She pointed to a pretty blonde-haired girl sitting in the front row.

"That's easy. Utah actually belonged to Mexico then. It didn't become a territory of the United States of America until 1849," the girl answered with an air of supreme confidence.

"And?" Hazel queried.

"And what?" Eliza faltered, suddenly less sure of herself.

"*Miss* Cannon, try for a moment—just a moment if you can—to look beyond your own parochial background. Contrary to what you might think, Utah wasn't the center of the universe. At least not then," she said to some chuckles from the rest of the class. "There *were* other things, very important things, going on. Tell me about those."

Eliza was silent.

"Anyone?" Hazel asked.

Tom raised his hand.

"Tom, tell us what Eliza has apparently overlooked," Hazel encouraged.

"The Gadsden Purchase in 1854," he answered without hesitation.

"Exactly," Hazel Whitcomb approved. "Utah was actually a rather minor part of the Union at that point. But whether the new territories of Utah and New Mexico would be considered slave states or free states *was* critically important to the balance of power in Congress. The Senate ratified the treaty with Mexico only after a prolonged and bitter debate. We'll talk about that tomorrow, and about why the South considered itself a victim of Northern aggrandizement. After all, slavery wasn't the only issue that divided North and South."

Mrs. Whitcomb paused, then announced, "That finishes our discussion for today." Some of the students, glancing at the wall clock and realizing that nearly half the class period remained, looked puzzled. She reached into her desk and pulled out a stack of blank "blue books." The class groaned in unison, knowing what was coming.

"That's right," she said as she started down the aisle, passing out the thin, paper-bound books. "Pop quiz time. You have," she paused, looking at the clock, "twenty-five minutes to finish the test. It's essay, of course. Answer any three of the questions on the board. Extra credit if you can answer four correctly." Hazel returned to the front of the class and slid back a section of blackboard to reveal five neatly lettered questions based on the week's homework assignment.

Eliza's mouth tightened. She and Tom van Sloten were running a close contest to become class valedictorian. She simply couldn't afford to lose a single point to her chief competition. If only she'd stayed home and studied last night instead of sneaking out and going on that date with Bill Richards . . . Eliza shook her head. It had been worth it, she decided. The captain of

East's basketball team was definitely worth the risk of getting caught. Everyone said what a striking couple they made. She had made sure he had a really good time. The Richardses always gave the fanciest New Year's Eve party in all of Federal Heights. She hoped and prayed he would ask her to be his date for the exclusive event.

"Time's up," Hazel announced as she began collecting the exam booklets. "Eliza, and you too, Tom: I'd like to talk with you right after school. Here. It won't take long," she added as she caught Tom's worried look. "I promise you won't be late for work. Or you for cheerleader practice either, Eliza."

Hazel had a brief moment of solitude as the room emptied and locker doors began to bang in the hallway, filling the air with a metallic cacophony. She erased the pop quiz questions and stowed the blue books in her briefcase for grading later that evening. One of the office secretaries bustled into the room and passed her a message on a pink memo sheet. It had a single, curt line in Major Garrison's meticulous handwriting. *Mrs. Whitcomb: See me in my office immediately after school.*

Hazel shrugged. Eliza and Tom would have to wait.

Tom followed Eliza out of Mrs. Whitcomb's class. The most popular girl in the senior class, Eliza was always surrounded by a fawning coterie. One of her friends glanced at Tom and snickered as he walked by the knot of chattering females. It was a painful reminder of the time he had first seen Eliza. They were both new sophomores at East. On an impulse, he had asked her to go with him for ice cream at Snelgrove's. She had looked him up and down, taking in his shabby clothes and shaking her head. "I don't think so, Tom. It just wouldn't be—you know—*right*." She hadn't even bothered to offer an excuse. Like *Oh, I'm so sorry, Tom, but I already have a date*. Or even *I'm busy*. It was just a flat no. "Sorry I even asked," he had muttered and stalked off. He could still remember one of her friends simpering, "Oh, Eliza, what on earth would make someone like *him* . . . ?"

Even now, Tom reddened at the memory of the casual brush-off.

Hazel reported to the administration offices as soon as the last class of the day was dismissed. "I've been summoned," she informed the secretary, who was clacking away on an old typewriter.

"Oh, Mrs. Whitcomb. The Dean will be with you in a moment," she promised.

Hazel sat down, glancing at her wristwatch. Ten minutes later, the door to Garrison's office swung open and he crooked his finger at her. "Ah, Mrs. Whitcomb. Do come in."

He seated himself behind a large desk that was positioned on a slightly elevated platform. "Sit down," Garrison ordered, pointing to a straight-backed wooden chair in front of the desk. The desktop was immaculate, empty except for a single manila folder and two pencils precisely aligned parallel to its edges. Reading upside down, Hazel saw it was her personnel file. She waited, curious as to how Garrison had gotten her file, not to mention why.

Garrison stared down at her, absently stroking his neatly trimmed mustache. As she looked into his pale gray eyes, Hazel had the odd sensation that Phyllis Tregagle's childhood nemesis was fixing her with its flat, unblinking gaze. She shuddered involuntarily.

Garrison opened the file, finally breaking his intimidating silence. "Mrs. Whitcomb," he intoned, voice full of importance as he glanced down at the file and then stared at her. "It has come to my attention—needless to mention how—that there are some *irregularities* in your professional qualifications. Perhaps the school board is unaware of this, um, shall we say, 'serious deficiency'?" he added silkily.

Hazel pushed the door closed.

As requested, Tom had returned to Mrs. Whitcomb's classroom immediately after school. Her absence puzzled him. Eliza Cannon was also nowhere in sight. He waited fruitlessly for a few minutes, then finally scribbled a quick note on a scrap of paper and left it on her desk.

One last possibility, Tom thought as he gathered his books together and scampered up the steps to the third floor. He stopped just outside the door of the teachers' lounge. Its opaque glass panel obscured the room. He put his ear to the glass and listened for a moment. Nothing but silence.

Tom rapped on the door. To his surprise, it creaked open.

"Anybody here?" he called out.

No one answered. Tom hesitated. Surely a quick peek couldn't hurt. He stepped inside and peered around the corner.

The room was deserted. The coffee urn gurgled and moaned in the stillness.

Tom hastily scribbled another note: *Dear Mrs. Whitcomb: I'm sorry I missed you. I have to leave for work but I will try to see you after class on Monday.* He ripped it from his tablet and looked around for a place to leave it in plain sight. He tried propping his message against the urn, but the note kept sliding off the table onto the floor. Spying the chipped mug, he placed it on the paper. Heavily weighted by the coins, it secured the note firmly in place.

Satisfied, Tom turned to leave, feeling mildly guilty at his trespass. He spotted a nearly empty plate of cookies on the end table next to the old sofa. There were two left. His stomach rumbled. He hadn't had lunch. Should he . . . ? Surely they wouldn't miss one cookie! He chided himself for even thinking about it.

As Tom closed the lounge door, he saw a figure bent over a push broom at the opposite end of the hallway. It was Old Jake, the janitor.

"Hey, Jake!" he shouted. "Have you seen Mrs. Whitcomb?"

Jake shook his head. "Nope. Ain't seen her all day."

"Thanks anyway," Tom called back as he headed down the stairs. "If you see her, please tell her there's a note for her in the lounge."

Jake nodded once and went back to his sweeping.

Tom checked Mrs. Whitcomb's room again, but there was no sign she'd been back. His note was still there. As he hurried out the side door to the street, he passed the gymnasium. He could hear the rhythmic bounce of basketballs and the occasional clang of an errant shot against the iron rim. A year ago he had tried out for the junior varsity and actually made the first cut. To the disgust of the coach, he had had to quit the team in the middle of the season so he could get an after-school job. He glanced through the open doorway and saw the cheerleading squad practicing on the far end of the court. He could see Eliza Cannon, blonde hair gathered into a thick braid that bounced and swayed as she led the group in a peppy routine.

Maybe Eliza's friend was right. He shook his head at the long-ago insanity that had made him even think she might accept a date from someone like him.

Hazel's fury propelled her back to her classroom. She seethed at Garrison's imperious manner. She had wanted to shout, *Of course the principal knows that I don't have a teaching certificate! I'm taking classes at the University of Utah's Extension Division. I'll have everything finished by the end of next summer!*

True to form, he hadn't let her offer a word in explanation.

Eliza and Tom were, of course, long gone. She would have to give them the special scholarship materials on Monday.

CHAPTER ELEVEN
Saturday, December 16, 1933

Tom's anxiety was blossoming into full-blown panic. Giving his mother the food and utility money had almost drained the jar. A bit over five dollars was all that was left. Delivering the Dunford bread had added a little. But there was no work for him when he showed up at Rosenblatt's. He decided to spend the morning shopping for the Santa Claus presents and see how far he could stretch his meager budget.

He saw a sixty-piece box of Daniel Boone logs in the Salt Lake 5 & 10 Cent Store. Brand-new, they were only forty-five cents. He briefly considered them for Davey. He was a clever child, but fitting the notched logs together to make forts and cabins would probably require more dexterity than a three-year-old could manage. Tom finally settled on balsa-wood building blocks that he found in the downtown Woolworth's store. At thirty-nine cents for a forty-piece set, it didn't put a big dent in his budget.

Shopping for the older boys was even harder. Every kid he knew wanted a Flexible Flyer sled. Paul longed for one. The night before, Tom had thumbed through the Sears and Roebuck catalog. It featured a sleek but less expensive brand called the Flying Arrow. The catalog trumpeted, "WHEE! There she goes! WOW! What a ride! Goes like a flash, just as its name suggests. Its long racy lines not only give it greater speed but its patented flexible steering enables you to slide farther!" The least expensive sled cost $1.69.

Even small things like board games or a starter set of Tinker Toys all cost at least fifty cents. He knew Richard was saving for a bicycle, but—at nineteen dollars for a new one—filling *that* dream was out of the question. Jeannie was interested only in her appearance. That meant Clothes, with a capital C. Meaning Cost, too, he mused.

He groaned in frustration. Then he had a sudden inspiration. The boys' gifts didn't *have* to be brand-new, just in good condition. Maybe he could find something suitable in one of the numerous secondhand stores that dotted the city.

His brilliant thought was confirmed when he walked to the Salvation Army Industrial Store. The problem was, hundreds of others had had the same idea and acted much earlier. Moreover, becoming cautious as the Depression stretched on, people weren't donating much.

Tom tried the Assistance League's Thrift Shop with the same discouraging result. He stood in silence, staring numbly at the dismal offerings and trying to fight off despair. The few available items had been thoroughly picked over, leaving only dregs that even the poorest shoppers didn't want. Tom grimaced, recalling the motto Sarah so often recited to the family:

> Use it up.
> Wear it out.
> Make it do,
> Or do without.

Suddenly a wizened, diminutive old woman sidled up to him. "Pssst!" she hissed, standing on tiptoes to attract his attention. "I'm gonna tell you a secret," she whispered in his ear with the sly tones of a seasoned conspirator. "The good stuff—well, what there is of it," she harrumphed, "it goes really fast. What you gotta do is stick around until they bring out a new batch. Then be super quick! Young fella like you can grab it right then. Get it before someone else does!"

Grabbing was verboten in Tom's family. But maybe the old woman had a point. He loitered in the toy section for nearly an hour. Just as he was about to give up, the "Employees Only" door flew open, and a clerk pushed a loaded cart into the retail area.

Trying not to be too obvious, Tom edged closer to see what was on the cart. A wooden toy train lay right on top! It would be perfect for Paul. If only he could get to it first. He tried to guess where the clerk would deposit the train, positioning himself for the strike.

He was in luck! The clerk maneuvered the cart down the aisle where he was waiting and deposited the train on an adjacent shelf. Tom reached for it. Just as he was about to grasp his prize, he was roughly shouldered aside.

"Gimme that!" a large, burly man demanded, snatching the train.

"I was here first!" Tom protested. "This isn't fair!"

"Tough," his opponent sneered with a triumphant smirk. "Possession is nine-tenths of the law!"

Thrusting his chest out, he dared Tom to challenge him.

A thin, clawlike hand appeared from nowhere and grasped the man's arm with surprising strength. It was the old woman. "Put it down," she ordered.

He whirled, enraged. She stood her ground, staring at him. "Put it down," she repeated.

There was a moment of absolute silence. Tom would never know what unspoken message passed between them, but the man's eyes abruptly lost their dangerous glitter. Reddening, he averted his gaze from the old woman's fiercely determined face. Then he slowly put the train back in its place. Turning his back, he stomped off, muttering sullenly.

"Here. It's yours," the old woman pronounced as she placed the train in Tom's hands. "It needs a bit of fixing up, but I think it'll serve. You'll give it a good home. Pay for it over that way." She cocked her head, gesturing him in the right direction.

Too stunned to speak, Tom tucked the train set under his arm and started off. Then, recovering his composure and remembering his manners, he turned to thank her.

The aisle was empty.

CHAPTER TWELVE

Saturday afternoon, December 16, 1933

The toy train was turning out even better than expected. Humming Christmas carols, Tom bent to the task of restoring the set to mint condition. He sanded off the chipped paint, smoothing the nicks and gouges in the tiny cars. He fashioned sturdy new axles for the existing miniature wheels and replaced missing ones. Then he polished the natural wood and painstakingly applied a coat of clear lacquer. The whole train gleamed.

It looked great, he thought with satisfaction.

That left Richard and Jean. There had been no used bicycles in any of the thrift shops. He scoured want ads in the local newspaper. There were lots more items offered for sale than were wanted, including several bicycles. None was under five dollars. He picked up the phone and heard one of the neighbors gossiping with a friend. Half an hour later, when the four-party line was clear, he made a few calls in hopes of bargaining the price down. No luck. Only one, a twenty-four-inch girl's bicycle, was still available. He haggled half-heartedly, but the owner rejected his best offer of two dollars.

Sighing to himself, Tom realized there was only one used bicycle that was available. His own.

He retrieved his bicycle from the garage and studied it. In an extraordinary sacrifice that still amazed him, his parents had bought it for him almost six years ago. He had been saving pennies and nickels from his morning paper route, hoping to buy a used bike. The brand-new Elgin had been his pride and joy. A careful child, he had never had a major accident or left it out in the rain. Still, it showed the inevitable wear and tear of heavy use. Worse yet, Richard would recognize it immediately. That would wreck Tom's Santa cover right then and there.

There were no realistic alternatives. He hated to give up his prized possession. But if he could somehow disguise it . . .

Tom smiled to himself. Why hadn't he thought of it before? If a scraggly tree could be transformed and a toy train restored to pristine condition, why not a bicycle? Maybe he could somehow work out a deal.

Deciding that negotiating a business proposition required looking neat—if not exactly prosperous—he took off his sawdust-covered, paint-spattered pants and put on a clean pair of overalls. Then he pedaled to Eldridge's Bicycle and Mower Shop. The doorbell jingled as he pushed his bicycle into the brightly lit store. It smelled of machine oil, new leather, and high expectations.

Mr. Eldridge himself came out, wiping lubricant from his hands. "Tom!" he exclaimed cheerfully. "How nice to see you again! Finally ready to trade in that old bicycle? I've got a brand-new Elgin Falcon here. Streamlined style makes it look like a motorcycle."

Tom shook his head longingly as he admired the sleek Falcon. "I can't afford a new bicycle, Mr. Eldridge. But my younger brother Richard wants one more than just about anything in the world." He gulped. "Is there any way to fix up mine for him? Make it look different so he won't know?"

Mr. Eldridge cleared his throat. "I know how much that bicycle means to you, son. Henry worked really hard to get it. He's very proud of you, you know." Then he paused, considering Tom's plan. "There's not much time left 'til Christmas," he mused. "But business is a mite slow. You've taken excellent care of that 'cycle. It's basically in good shape. With a bit of work my boy and I could make it look brand-new. Replace a few parts, paint the frame and fenders, polish the wheels. That sort of thing."

"How much would that cost?" Tom asked, painfully aware of his dwindling cash.

Mr. Eldridge looked thoughtful. "It really needs a new seat, too. Those retail for $1.45. New grips run eleven cents each. Kickstand would be another twenty-three cents. With labor and parts, say maybe $2.50 total."

A budget buster. Tom's shoulders drooped.

"Tell you what," Mr. Eldridge suggested after a moment of silence. "This place is always a real mess after the holidays. You're a hard worker, and I can think of a number of things you could help with. Promise me eight hours— any time you can work them in—and you've got yourself a deal."

Tom could scarcely believe his good fortune. "Thanks, Mr. Eldridge! I'll make it up to you, I promise!"

"I know you will," Mr. Eldridge responded with a wink, looking at his calendar. "Let me check our work schedule. Christmas is a week from Monday. We'll be closed on Sunday, of course. How 'bout we have it ready for you the afternoon of the twenty-third? Saturday. Sound okay?" he asked, scribbling out a receipt.

"You bet!" Tom enthused, stuffing the bill into his pocket. He was already thinking about the last person on his list. Jean. She would be the hardest of all.

❧ CHAPTER THIRTEEN ☙

Saturday afternoon, December 16, 1933

Jean adored secrets. They were especially delicious when they were someone else's secrets. Tom was up to something. Her instincts screamed that her brother had Big Plans. He had been even more closed-mouthed than usual, acting edgy and short-tempered. He had actually grabbed her in that blowup over the stupid dishes! She smiled at her success in baiting Saint Tom.

Then there was that night when, pretending to be asleep on the sofa, she had seen Tom disappear into the dining room with Sarah and Hendrik. To her dismay they had shut the door, and all she could hear was soft, unintelligible murmuring. The muted conversation was punctuated once with a sharp rejoinder from her father, "Don't say that!" After another few minutes, they all came out. Keeping one eye closed and reminding herself to breathe the rhythms of deep sleep, Jean thought she saw dried tears on her mother's cheeks. Hendrik looked angry. Tom seemed crestfallen. Then, to pile mystery on top of mystery, he had sneaked out of the house after Sarah and Hendrik had gone to bed.

She had struggled to stay awake but woke the next morning with the smell of pine in her nostrils. A magnificent Christmas tree had appeared during the night! She had cornered Tom later and hinted at several possibilities, trying without success to trick him into disclosing his plans.

A born snoop, Jean loved Nancy Drew mysteries. She devoured every book in the library about the famous girl detective and had read most of them at least twice. Jean could imagine herself wheeling around town in Nancy's sporty roadster, top down, hair flying in the wind as she pursued wrongdoers and ferreted out crimes that had stumped the local police.

She decided to spy on Tom. That afternoon she followed him as he cycled to Eldridge's. *Nancy would be proud,* Jean thought as she skulked behind a tree. When Tom exited the store empty-handed she knew immediately what he had done.

He had sold his precious bicycle. But why?

Jean scurried home. The younger boys were all outside playing, making it an ideal time to investigate. She rarely ventured into their bedroom, but she had already decided to check it out before Tom returned.

He had fashioned a shelf to hold his few personal books. A small collection, fewer than half a dozen volumes, chronicled his maturing tastes. Alfred Payson Terhune's *Lad, a Dog* and *Frog, the Horse Who Knew No Master*. Those were earlier birthday presents from their parents. There was a worn copy of *Black Beauty*. Jean felt a stab of guilt at that one. When Tom was in sixth grade, he had bought it for a friend's birthday and read it before the party, taking great care not to wrinkle the cover. *Let me read it too,* she implored. He was reluctant; she persisted. When he finally relented, she carted it off to the table and promptly got a grease spot on it. It was one of the few times she had seen him truly angry. He bought a new one for the friend and kept the damaged copy himself. She pulled the book out and smiled. The spot was still visible.

The next book was an odd choice: Gray and Jenkins's *Latin for Today*. Jean couldn't imagine spending money on a Latin book, of all things! She found a receipt tucked inside the cover. Twenty-five cents from Utah-Idaho

School Supply. The last book was a thick tome, *Les Misérables*, by some guy named Victor Hugo. *Who wants to read something miserable?* Jean wondered. *Especially these days!* She pulled it from the shelf and opened it. There was a brief inscription inside. "To Tom, With best regards. May this be the first of many. Fondly, Sam and Gus." Many what? She couldn't recall that Tom ever mentioned having friends named Sam and Gus.

There was a bookmark stuck inside. It was embossed, "Zion's Book Store, 28 East First South, Salt Lake City. Gus Weller, proprietor." One mystery solved. The owner of Zion's Books, Gus Weller, was probably the Gus of "Sam and Gus." That made sense; the bookstore was less than a block from Rosenblatt's, the upscale department store where Tom worked part-time as a stock boy. But who was Sam?

In her best girl-detective fashion, Jean held the book by its covers and shook it. A square of heavily creased and folded yellow notepaper fluttered to the floor. Jean opened it and sucked in her breath.

It was some sort of list. A Christmas list, by the look of it.

Christmas tree	$ .25
Utilities, rent, etc.	$9.00
Dinner	$3.00
Presents	$3.00
Jean	
(Richard) ?	
~~Paul~~	
~~David~~	
Contingencies	$ .98

Jean's face fell. Three dollars for everyone. And her name wasn't crossed off yet.

She refolded the list, putting it and the bookmark back inside *Les Misérables*. As she tried to approximate their original positions, she mentally scolded herself for not noting the exact spots in the first place. *I should have been more careful*, she thought. *Nancy wouldn't have made that mistake.*

Jean peered under Tom's bed. A dust bunny drifted out and settled on the floor beside the bunk. *No hidden presents there*, she thought with a stab of disappointment.

She felt under his pillow and slid her hand under the mattress. Nothing.

Jean moved to the dresser and opened Tom's drawer. Shirts, underwear, socks, all arranged in neat stacks. She reached toward the back. Her exploring fingers encountered a cool, smooth surface. It clinked when she touched it. *It's his bank!* she thought, thrilled at the discovery. She removed the glass jar and surveyed its contents, surprised at how little he had saved. *I've got a lot more*, she thought smugly as she put it back in the exact spot so he would never know she'd been snooping.

There was no closet on the sleeping porch, so the boys hung their clothes on pegs by the door. Jean removed an old pair of Tom's pants. They smelled odd, a sharp, pungent odor that reminded her of fingernail polish remover. She probed the pockets but found nothing. Then something spilled from the rolled-up cuffs. She knelt, examining the fine powder. Sawdust! Why would Tom have sawdust in his pants, of all things? It just didn't make sense. What in the world was he up to?

❧ CHAPTER FOURTEEN ❧

Saturday afternoon, December 16, 1933

J ean stormed downtown. She didn't know what the inscription inside *Les Misérables* meant, but she intended to find out. The strange book might even be a clue to the mystery. After all, Tom's Christmas list had been hidden in it.

She marched past Rosenblatt's, ignoring the store's windows with their tasteful holiday décor. This time she didn't so much as glance at the expensively dressed mannequins.

Jean checked the number: 28 East First South. This was it. Weller's famous bookstore. She had never been inside, but she didn't hesitate. Pushing the door open, she encountered a square-jawed man with a high forehead and an unruly thatch of carrot-colored hair. Wire-rimmed spectacles perched at the end of his long nose. He was dressed for the festive season in a cheerful red-and-green-striped shirt, mismatched plaid tie, and sequined suspenders that sparkled in the colored lights draped around the store.

"*Mister* Weller?" Jean inquired with a half-hearted attempt at courtesy. "Mr. *Gus* Weller?"

"Ya? Could I help?" he responded in a heavy German accent.

She didn't mince words. "I'm Jean van Sloten. Why did you give Tom a miserable book?"

Her hapless target looked nonplussed. "A 'miserable book'? I haf no idea vat you mean by dis, young lady."

"You gave him one. *Les Misérables*," she insisted, pronouncing it "less miserables."

"You and some guy named Sam wrote in it," she continued and quoted the inscription exactly.

The light dawned. "Ah! So! You're Tom's sister!" Gus looked relieved. "Actually it vas my son, dat's young Sam, who had da idea to gif him dat book. Tom, sometimes he comes here on his vay home from Rosenblatt's. He and Sam haf become goot friends. By the vay, da title of dis book is in French. It's pronounced 'lay mee-zay-rob.'"

"Whatever," Jean snorted. "So may I talk to this 'Young Sam'?"

"Of course," Gus agreed equably. "Come mit me," he gestured. "Young Sam's vorking in da back."

Jean followed him into a large, disorderly room that was stacked with books from floor to ceiling. In the middle of this chaos a handsome man in his mid-twenties chewed on a pencil, then scribbled notations on a clipboard.

"Sam!" Gus interrupted. "Ve haf a visitor. Dis is Jean van Sloten. Tom's older sister."

Jean didn't correct him.

Young Sam stuck out his hand in welcome, a big grin spreading across his face. "Glad to meet you," he enthused. "Tom's told me a lot about you."

"Well, I don't know anything about *you!*" Jean shot back. "But I'm about to find out."

"Whoa! What have I done to ruffle your feathers, Miss Jean?" Sam replied.

Smelling a confrontation, Gus beat a hasty retreat.

"I have a mystery that needs solving," Jean cut to the point as she glared at the bemused Sam. "And I think you're part of it, Young Mr. Weller!"

"So what is this mystery, Jean?"

"You gave my brother *Les Misérables*," she stated, pronouncing the name flawlessly this time.

"Yes indeed I did," Sam replied in a mild tone. "What of it?"

Jean was undeterred. "I want to know *why*. Why you'd do such a thing. What you meant by what you and Gus—Mr. Weller—wrote in it."

"Several years ago when I was at the university, I served as a volunteer assistant librarian at Roosevelt Junior High. I love books. Always have. It runs in our family," Sam digressed as he tenderly caressed an old volume. "I have a three-year-old son, Tony." Lost in his reverie, Sam missed the disappointment that momentarily flitted across Jean's face.

"I read to Tony every night," Sam mused. "Not baby stories. Good stuff like Shakespeare. I could swear he understands it. Some people just do, you know."

Sam continued. "Your brother Tom is one of those rare individuals who's born with an insatiable love of learning. He came into the library the first day of school. Just stood there in wonder, looking around at all the books. Never said a word, but the expression on his face—well, it was almost rapturous. Eventually Tom pulled a fat book off the shelf and sat down to read. In those days the kids weren't allowed to check out books. Classes started at 8:30 A.M. So Tom came in every day at 8:00 and read that thing all the way through. It was *Les Misérables*.

"One day I asked him why he had picked that particular book. It isn't an easy read, you know. Tom looked up at me and said simply, 'Because it's the biggest one on the shelf.' From then on, I helped him select some of the best books. The guy has an amazing memory. He never forgets anything. When I started working here at the store, Dad and I invited him to visit. He's been coming ever since. Not real often, but when he does we always chat together for a while."

"About what?"

"Oh, lots of things. Religion. Philosophy. Politics. American history. You name it, we've talked about it."

Jean was astonished. She simply couldn't imagine Tom talking that much. "So where does *Les Misérables* come in?"

"All Tom wants is books. Last May Dad and I gave it to him for his birthday. Turning sixteen's a real landmark, you know, next to twenty-one. And *Les Misérables* was his first true love. The first of anything is always special," he added softly.

Sam took Jean by the arm. "Come on," he urged, pulling her toward the doorway. "I want to show you something."

Sam turned down another hallway, Jean in tow. Every wall was stacked with books. One room led to another. The store was a veritable warren, a maze of haphazardly connected rooms and cubbyholes that smelled of dust and old paper and faraway places.

"Every time some space on the block becomes available, Dad buys it," Sam explained. "Not everything fronts on the street, but we've pulled out walls and rewired the rooms. Doesn't look all that great, but it works."

Sam led her down a corridor so narrow that they had to turn sideways to pass through. It opened into an anteroom faced by a solid-looking steel door.

"This is the 'Inner Sanctum,'" he grinned, eyes twinkling. "And pray tell me, Miss Jean, what do you think lies beyond that door?"

Jean shivered. Given the musty smells of the place, she wasn't sure she wanted to know.

Sam pulled out a fat key chain and unlocked the door. "This is the best place in the store," he said with obvious pride as it clicked open. "Come on in."

It was a vaulted room lined with books of every description. Three or four comfortable overstuffed chairs with side tables and shaded reading lamps were scattered around a fine oriental rug.

"This is reserved for our best customers," Sam explained. "Sort of a club for bibliophiles. Book lovers. It's also where we keep our really valuable stock. Rare books and memorabilia, things like Western Americana and early Utah historical items."

Jean was mesmerized.

"Your brother has his own spot here," Sam continued. "Not for rare stuff, of course," he added hastily. "Dad and I gave him a shelf where he keeps the books he's buying a bit at a time."

Sam walked over to a modest collection. "Machiavelli's *The Prince. The Complete Works of William Shakespeare.* Modern Library editions of *The Odyssey* and *The Iliad.* They're not expensive, of course. But Tom wants to have them. He puts down a quarter or two every few weeks. At least he used to," Sam corrected himself. "When times weren't so tight. I haven't seen him for a while. But Dad and I keep the books waiting for him. Someday they'll be his."

Jean was puzzled. "Why doesn't he just check them out of the library like everybody else does?"

Sam laughed. "Having something that's your very own, especially like a book or piece of art, is special to guys like Dad and me. Tom's just getting started. We put things back here that we think he'd like. Sort of a 'lay-away' program, but for books instead of dresses."

Jean winced a little at the mention of buying clothing in installments. "What's the best thing he's saving for?" she asked.

"That's easy," Sam answered without hesitating. "This one." He reached for a small volume. "It's a 1926 First Edition of Will Durant's *The Story of Philosophy*. Tom likes this particular book because he felt the introduction really spoke directly to him. Would you like me to read it to you?"

Jean shrugged as Sam opened the book. "Mr. Durant says, 'So much of our lives is meaningless, a self-cancelling vacillation and futility; we strive with the chaos about us and within; but we would believe all the while that there is something vital and significant in us, could we but decipher our own souls.'"

Sam fixed Jean with a meaningful look. "Have you ever wanted to decipher your own soul, Jean? I know I have. Tom and I've talked about that too. There's more. Durant continues, 'We want . . . to pull ourselves up out of the maelstrom of daily circumstance. We want to know that the little things are little, and the big things big, before it is too late; we want to see things now as they will seem forever—in the light of eternity.' Don't you want to know what's really important in life?"

Jean laughed uneasily.

Sam closed the book and put it back on Tom's shelf. "This is a particularly fine item, Jean. That's partly because it's in its original dust jacket or 'D.J.' Do you know what a First Edition is?"

Jean shook her head.

"It's the first limited press run of a book," Sam explained. "If a book is successful and goes into a second printing or more, its 'First Edition' can become quite valuable. Of course, this one isn't signed and dated by the author. If it were, it would be even more expensive."

"And just what does 'expensive' mean?" Jean asked hesitantly. She knew how much an expensive outfit like the one she hoped to buy for the New Year's Eve party cost.

Sam told her.

Jean gasped, shocked that such a plain little book could cost more than a new dress plus matching shoes and purse all put together.

Her jaw clenched as she remembered Tom's Christmas list. Three dollars for all his gifts combined.

❧ CHAPTER FIFTEEN ❧
Sunday morning, December 17, 1933

I t was one of Hendrik's few pleasurable moments. He buried his nose in the freshly starched white shirt that Sarah washed and pressed each week, inhaling its sweet fragrance. He relished putting on the clean garment, mellowed with age to a soft ivory. He knotted his tie in a meticulous four-in-hand, then brushed the jacket of his Sunday-best outfit, a serviceable but worn navy blue suit. The suit was shiny from too many pressings, but, he reminded himself gratefully, it still had a lot of good wear left in it. Checking himself in the small bathroom mirror, he nodded with satisfaction.

The last act of this Sunday morning ritual was his favorite. He reached into the dresser and removed the cheap silver-plated pocket watch he had inherited from his father. The old watch had belonged to his Dutch namesake, Grandfather Hendrik. He wound the stem, checked the time, and placed the watch in his vest pocket.

"You look really nice, sweetheart," Sarah commented as she watched him adjust his broad-brimmed fedora at a jaunty angle. "Except for that old tie. It looks a bit tatty. Why aren't you wearing your favorite, that navy-and-red-striped regimental the boys gave you for your birthday?"

"I don't have it anymore, Sarah," Hendrik confessed.

"You don't *have* it anymore? What in the world . . . How can anyone lose a necktie, for heaven's sake!"

"I didn't lose it. I sort of . . . well, it's out on what I suppose you might call a 'permanent loan.'"

"Art galleries and museums lend each other paintings, Henry, but I never heard of someone loaning out a necktie!"

"Three weeks ago the church leaders appointed Fred Stockdale to serve as my new assistant in the Sunday school. Today is our first leadership conference with one of the local congregations. We'll be sitting in front, on the rostrum along with all the other top church leaders."

Sarah waited, not understanding what that had to do with the missing tie.

"After the Sunday school board meeting early this week, Fred drew me aside and told me he couldn't attend the conference. I pressed him for a reason, and he finally admitted it was because he didn't have a suit and tie. I don't have an extra suit, but I do have two ties. So . . ." he grinned a bit sheepishly, "Brother Fred will come in a white shirt, sweater, and a rather handsome regimental tie."

Sarah had to smile. Even in their poverty, Hendrik never failed to share whatever he had. "We'll meet you at the Stanfords' home after church, Henry—the children are really looking forward to it. So am I! It was very generous of the Stanfords to invite all the officers and their families for Sunday dinner."

"Must be thirty people, at least," Henry marveled. "Dinner for that many would cost a small fortune. But people still have to heat their homes and buy coal, so if anyone can afford a dinner like that, the Stanfords could."

Sarah didn't mention their own underpaid bill.

♣

At the closing bell, children spilled out of the church and filled the sidewalks in front of the venerable old building. A few snowballs splatted on the pavement to squeals of mock outrage.

Tom smiled through chattering teeth, clutching his thin jacket for the little warmth it provided. He stomped his feet as he waited for the family to gather for the considerable walk up the hill to the Stanfords' elegant home in the Garden Park area.

One of the neighborhood matrons, a nosy woman whom Tom struggled not to dislike, accosted him. "Thomas van Sloten!" she scolded as she picked at his sleeve. "You should be wearing your winter coat. You'll catch your death in weather like this!"

Sarah came to Tom's side. "He doesn't have one, Mrs. Peterson."

The older woman had the grace to look embarrassed. "I apologize, Tom. I—I guess I just didn't think . . ."

Tom tried to paste a smile of forgiveness on his face. It came out more like a grimace. "That's okay, Mrs. Peterson. You didn't mean any harm."

Just then Jean and the boys materialized, so the family began the trek up the hill, the little boys shouting and pelting each other with snowballs.

When they reached their destination, all Tom could do was gawk at the

Stanfords' house. "Jeannie," he whispered, "are the homes in Federal Heights as big as this?"

"Bigger. At least some of them are," she nodded, even looking impressed herself.

Tom thought about the fancy dress. No wonder Jean yearned for an elegant outfit, if she'd been invited to a New Year's Eve party at a place like this!

The Stanfords met them at the large double door; behind them, the tantalizing scent of roasting meat filled the air. "Come in, come in!" they urged. Jeannie stared up at the high arched ceilings. "Someday I'm going to live in a house just like this one," she breathed to Tom in awe.

"Shh!" Tom hissed, embarrassed at his sister's undisguised envy.

"Shh yourself!" she retorted in a fierce whisper. "I *will!* You'll see!"

Tom rolled his eyeballs in disgust.

The enormous dining room seated twenty with room to spare. Along with Rachel, the Stanfords' oldest daughter, Tom was invited to sit with the church leaders and their wives. He felt a prick of satisfaction when Jeannie was assigned to the children's tables downstairs.

They all knelt on the thick carpeting for a blessing on the food, then were seated as their host carved the roast with a skill evidently born of long practice.

Tom had never seen so much silverware. He counted at least three forks, three spoons, and two knives at each place setting, plus another odd-shaped spoon positioned above each of the large dinner plates. One fork, one spoon, he could handle that. But all those other implements? He watched Rachel and did exactly as she did.

He couldn't remember ever having eaten such a feast. Roast beef, a large helping of mashed potatoes smothered with pan gravy, canned corn and peas, homemade rolls with two kinds of jam, apple pie and cheese or vanilla ice cream for dessert. *So that's what the funny-looking spoon is for*, Tom concluded.

Everyone ate until they couldn't down another bite.

"Oh, I hurt so good!" Hendrik groaned aloud as everyone burst out laughing.

"That's the nicest compliment I've ever had," Mrs. Stanford approved, making Hendrik blush.

"I move we thank the Stanfords for their wonderful hospitality and dismiss this gathering for an afternoon nap before evening services," Sarah added. She was followed by a unanimous chorus of "I second the motion!"

As the van Slotens traipsed back down the hill, Tom couldn't help but think about their own meager Christmas. Jeannie was always talking about how she wanted to move up in the world. Maybe she had a point.

CHAPTER SIXTEEN

Monday morning, December 18, 1933

East High vibrated with the sounds of slamming locker doors and excited chatter. The short pre-Christmas week spawned a happy, carefree anticipation scarcely dampened by the loud bell warning that the first class period would start in five minutes.

"Hey, Tom!" Louie Chaffos and Dean Lindsay shouted as they headed down the hall to their first class of the day. Tom grinned and waved. Things were going so smoothly with his secret plans that he was actually beginning to enjoy the holiday spirit. His smile vanished as he spied Jean flirting and batting her eyelashes at two boys from the junior class. They appeared enchanted, immensely flattered by her coy attentions.

"You have your ways, and I have mine," her defiant retort echoed in his mind. Oh, yes, Jean did have her ways. He had just seen a graphic demonstration of exactly what she meant.

Tom hurried toward his own locker. Even from a distance he could see the pink note jammed into its vents. He tore it open. THOMAS VAN SLOTEN: REPORT TO THE PRINCIPAL'S OFFICE **IMMEDIATELY** WHEN YOU GET TO SCHOOL.

What—! Out of reflex he looked at the hall clock: 7:58 A.M. Two minutes until his first period English class.

Tom trotted through the rapidly diminishing throngs of students and headed for the offices on the main floor. He handed the note to the receptionist with a quizzical look.

"Thomas van Sloten," the receptionist nodded. "Walk right back to Dr. Schneider's office. Go on in. They're waiting for you."

They? "Who's they?"

She shook her head and looked away without answering.

Mystified, Tom obeyed. He noticed a uniformed police officer sitting in the waiting room outside the principal's office. The man was paging through an old *National Scholastic* magazine, looking thoroughly bored.

"Tom, come in," Dr. Schneider called to him. "Please shut the door."

Tom closed the door and turned toward the principal. He gave an involuntary start when he saw they weren't alone. Mr. Siddons, white-faced and grim, was standing across the desk from the principal. Next to him, shuffling his feet and twisting his cap in his dirt-encrusted hands, was Old Jake. He was staring at the floor. Jake's lips were moving soundlessly. Dean Garrison stood ramrod straight with his back to the window, arms folded across his chest. A scarcely concealed look of vindication contorted his face into a self-righteous smirk.

"Thomas," Dr. Schneider began without preamble, "we have a problem. It seems you may be able to help us."

"Sure, Dr. Schneider, I'll do my best. What's the problem?" Tom's scalp prickled at the strange atmosphere in the office. He tried to keep his voice steady.

Dr. Schneider sighed. "I'll be blunt. Some money's gone missing."

Tom had a sudden sense of foreboding. "Money? Missing? What happened?"

The principal turned to Dean Garrison.

"We thought perhaps you, Tom, could enlighten us, hmm?" Garrison purred.

"I don't understand."

"I think perhaps you do." Garrison waggled his finger at Tom. "The coffee money in the teachers' lounge. It disappeared sometime between Friday after school and early this morning. *I* thought perhaps Jim here did what I explicitly ordered him to do, namely, take the damned money and put it in the safe. Then we wouldn't have this little problem. But it seems you didn't do that, now, did you, Jim?" His tone said, *I told you so.*

Siddons shook his head.

Garrison continued, "You see, Tom, there are only three people who have a full set of keys and unrestricted access to the building. That's Dr. Schneider, of course. Myself as Acting Vice Principal. And the janitor, Old Jake."

He looked at Jake. "Tell everyone what you told me."

"Do—do I hafta?" Jake stammered.

"Of course you do! Don't be silly," Garrison snapped.

Jake mumbled something unintelligible.

"Speak up, man!" Garrison bit off his words.

"Last Friday I wuz up on th' third floor, sweepin' th' hallway after school. Ya know how messy kids are, they don't—"

"Get on with it, Jake!" Garrison gestured impatiently.

"Well, as I sez, I wuz sweepin' up when I saw him." Jake pointed at Tom. "*Him.* Tom van Sloten. He wuz comin' outta th' teachers' lounge. Ain't no students s'posed tuh be in there, either."

"I can explain everything!" Tom interrupted.

"You'll have your chance, Tom," Dr. Schneider put in.

"I—I was just trying to find Mrs. Whitcomb!" Tom insisted, voice rising. "She asked me to see her immediately after school. She said it was really important. I went to her classroom after the last period, but she wasn't there. Then it occurred to me maybe she was upstairs in the lounge. So I—" he faltered, "I guess I shouldn't have. I mean, we all know students aren't allowed in there. But the door was unlocked and—and I went in. Just for a minute, that's all. Mrs. Whitcomb wasn't there, so I left a note."

"Note? You didn't say anything about a note," Dr. Schneider said, eyeing Garrison.

"*I* wasn't aware of any note," Garrison responded icily. "Jake, did you find a note in the lounge?"

Jake shook his head.

"I'm not lying! I'm telling you the truth! I didn't take any money!" Tom protested. "I've never stolen anything in my life. Not even as much as an old stale cookie that didn't belong to me!"

Tom's head whirled, and he heard a loud buzzing in his ears as the room started to spin. His vision clouded, then faded as he sagged to the floor. The blood rushed back to his head. Blinking rapidly, he looked up and found himself staring at a ring of concerned faces.

Garrison leaned over and whispered into Tom's still-buzzing ear. "Tom, you broke the rules. You went into an area that's strictly off-limits. Maybe you thought you could get away with it because you're a good student. But no one—*no one*—is above the law here at East. Breaking rules must have consequences. And by the way, there's one other thing. You left the evidence behind. For a smart kid, that was really pretty stupid."

"Evidence?" Tom mumbled, thick-tongued.

"Evidence. The mug, of course. We'll be turning it over to the police."

"Police?" Tom's mind was moving in slow motion.

"I'm sorry, Tom," Dr. Schneider apologized, sounding genuinely regretful, "but you're going to have to go downtown." He opened the office door and beckoned to the waiting patrolman, handing him a paper bag that contained the incriminating mug.

"I don't believe this," Tom spluttered. "This is unreal . . ." He pinched himself. It hurt.

"Cuff him?" Garrison asked hopefully.

"I don't think that's necessary. Not unless he resists," the patrolman answered in a tolerant voice. "You won't give me any trouble, now, will you, son?"

Numb with shock, Tom shook his head. The patrolman took his arm and escorted him toward the door. Garrison spun on his heel and marched out.

"I loathe that son of a—," Siddons ground through clenched teeth.

"Easy, Jim! He was only doing his duty," Dr. Schneider countered.

"Yeah, I suppose, but does he have to enjoy it so much?"

"Garrison takes his responsibilities very seriously, Jim. Some of us could use a little more of that attitude."

Siddons winced. "What's going to happen to Tom?"

"That depends."

"What do you mean, 'that depends'?"

"What happens to a kid who breaks the law actually varies quite a bit. I gather there's a lot of leeway in how different cases are handled. Old Judge Goates retired earlier this year. There's a new judge, Rulon Clark, in charge of the juvenile court now. He seems to be more focused on treatment and rehabilitation than on punishing the kids. We've had a couple of cases this fall. One kid had already been in trouble with the law several times. He went straight to the Youth Detention Center down on Twenty-First South and Second East. They strip the kids, issue them detention shirt and pants, and keep them overnight. Or until the juvenile probation officer can file his report."

Siddons shuddered.

"I'm guessing that won't happen to Tom," Schneider continued. "The patrolman already asked me about his background. You know, school record, family, that sort of thing. I told him Tom was a top student and that his family, although they're really poor, seem to be decent, law-abiding citizens. The officer took a bunch of notes. The chief of the youth bureau downtown, Sergeant Bleyle—"

"I know him!" Siddons interrupted. "He's a tough guy. Law and order type. Likes to intimidate the kids. He says it helps soften 'em up. He's perfected the act and says nine times out of ten it works beautifully."

Schneider nodded. "The other case we had was a kid who got in a minor scrape. Never been in trouble before. Bleyle and Judge Clark scared the daylights out of him! Really taught him a lesson. I'm guessing that if Tom accepts full responsibility for what he's done and takes it like a man, he'll probably get off with a stern lecture and a fine."

CHAPTER SEVENTEEN

Monday morning, December 18, 1933

Mercifully, the halls were empty by now, so no classmates would see his disgrace. The policeman led an unresisting Tom to a patrol car that was double-parked in front of the school's main entrance. Opening the rear door, he gestured Tom into a backseat that was separated from the front by a wire mesh grill. Immediately claustrophobic, Tom tried to roll the window down. It didn't budge. He depressed the door handle and found it didn't open from the inside.

The ride downtown passed in a blur. The police station was in a large red brick building on the corner of First South and State Street. The main hall was a jumble of untidy desks, jangling phones, and harried people rushing back and forth in an atmosphere of great urgency. "Would you like me to call your parents?" the arresting officer asked, not unkindly.

"My mom's at home. Dad's probably still in the job line," Tom replied, trying to keep the terror out of his voice as he gave his address and home phone number. The patrolman passed the information to a secretary and began filling out a report, consulting his notepad as he recorded the crime's details. With Tom in tow he stopped at the evidence room, placed the mug in a special bag, and instructed the clerk to have it dusted and checked for fingerprints. Then he escorted Tom to the cramped cubicle that served as Sergeant Bleyle's office.

"This is Sergeant Bleyle, Tom. He's in charge of the Youth Division." The patrolman handed the new file to a stern-looking officer in an immaculate uniform. More than his sergeant's stripes and service hashes halfway up to his elbow, his manner radiated authority.

Bleyle glowered at Tom. "Sit down," he commanded, gesturing at a wooden chair that faced the desk. He read the file in silence, then leaned back. "Anything you want to tell me, son?"

"Yessir," Tom replied, voice trembling. "I didn't do it."

The officer stared back with a look that said, *That's what they all say*.

Tom stared back.

Bleyle heaved a deep theatrical sigh. "I don't believe in mollycoddling kids, Tom. I leave that up to the juvenile court and its 'treatment and rehabilitation,'" he snorted scornfully. "There *are* special rules for juveniles. But I'm not averse to overlooking them in difficult cases."

He called in his clerk. "Take van Sloten down and have him mugged and fingerprinted," he ordered. "Let him see how criminals are treated."

The police photographer took Tom's mug shot, full front view and profile. Tom blinked as the camera's harsh flash bored two incandescent holes into his dazed brain. Another officer pulled out a pad of black ink and smeared Tom's fingers across it, then took each one and pressed it firmly onto a cardboard file. The officer handed Tom an old rag. Tom did the best he could to wipe the ink from his hands. He felt as though the stain seeped into his very soul.

The clerk returned Tom to Bleyle's office.

"Well, Tom?" Bleyle grated. "Let's give this one more try."

"I told you the truth. I swear it!" Tom insisted.

Bleyle shook his head as a secretary peered into the cubicle and announced, "His mother is here."

"Have her wait," Bleyle snapped as he turned back to Tom. "You're in some real deep trouble, son. Want to change your story and tell me what really happened?"

"I didn't do it, Sergeant Bleyle," Tom repeated.

"Make it easy on yourself. 'Fess up. After all, the amount you took," Bleyle paused, checking the report, "estimated here at 'slightly over five dollars,' isn't much. That means we're talking misdemeanor here, not a major felony. You're a juvenile and a first-time offender. Chances are you'd get off with probation and giving the money back. Once you turned eighteen, it probably wouldn't even be part of your permanent record. Come on, Tom," he wheedled. "Save yourself some trouble and me a lot of paperwork."

Tom shook his head in disbelief.

"Okay, Tom," Bleyle scowled. "Go ahead and be a tough guy. Since you won't come clean and admit what you've done, you'll have to post bail in the amount of five dollars. Or else go to juvenile detention. If for some reason the judge lets you go home instead—which I doubt—we'll apply the five bucks to your restitution or fine. You have to come up with the money *now* or go to jail."

He waited. Tom kept silent.

Bleyle rose and stuck the file under his arm. "Have it your way. Come with me," he gestured.

"Where are you taking me? To jail?" Tom queried, his voice rising in fear.

"Naw," Bleyle sneered. "Not to jail. To court. Juvie. Christmas is coming, and the judge will want to take care of this little matter right here and now."

Sarah paced up and down in the waiting room. When Sergeant Bleyle appeared with Tom, she burst into tears.

"Mom!" Tom broke down and started to cry. "I didn't do it! They said I did, but I didn't!"

Sarah held her weeping son. "Hush now, Tom. We need to get hold of ourselves. Crying isn't going to do one bit of good." She gulped through her tears as she looked over Tom's shoulder at Sergeant Bleyle and asked, "What happens now?"

"Your son's going to the City and County Building to be arraigned in juvenile court, ma'am. At this stage it's really just a formality. He'll enter his plea to the charges. You know—guilty or not guilty. Then the judge will probably release him to your custody. You can ride with us if you like."

Sarah nodded dumbly and followed Bleyle and Tom to the squad car. Bleyle drove in silence, then parked in front of the gray granite building that Salt Lake City shared with the county. The slot was clearly marked "NO PARKING." He paid it no attention.

Bleyle led Tom and Sarah past a security guard to a creaky elevator that clanked and groaned as it slowly ascended to the fifth floor. When it finally stopped, the elderly operator pulled the folding metal gate back, and they stepped into a long, drafty hallway that was lined with wooden benches.

"It—it's *cold!*" Tom shivered.

"Sure is," Bleyle agreed. "Cold as all get-out in the winter and hotter 'n' Hades in the summer. We call it 'The Pigeon Loft.' You can see why." He pointed to a dirty window. A half-dozen pigeons were perched on the sill, heads bobbing and jerking as they strutted about gurgling and cooing at each other. Years' worth of droppings whitened the ledge.

"You'll need to wait right here," Bleyle said, gesturing at a wooden bench outside a tall door. A gold-lettered sign on the door read: *JUVENILE COURT. Judge Rulon Clark, presiding.* "This may take a while," he acknowledged.

Sarah sat in rigid silence. Tom fidgeted, heart racing with apprehension as he vainly tried to get comfortable on the hard bench. The whole thing was surreal, like a waking nightmare. He stared at his hands. They seemed detached from his body, as though they belonged to someone else.

The elevator creaked open, and Hendrik shuffled down the hall, breathing hard.

"Tom!" Hendrik looked mortified. "How could—"

"I didn't do it, Dad! I swear I didn't!"

The door to juvenile court banged open before Hendrik could respond to Tom's denial. A clerk stuck his head out and bawled, "THE STATE OF UTAH IN THE INTEREST OF THOMAS VAN SLOTEN!!"

The family followed the clerk and seated themselves on the hard wooden chairs at the front of the half-empty courtroom. Four rows faced a triangular-shaped desk. A distinguished-looking man in a business suit sat behind the desk perusing Tom's file.

He glanced up. "The accused will rise."

Hendrik blanched at the term. Tom stood up, head bowed.

"The clerk will read the charges," Judge Clark ordered.

The clerk, thumbing through pages of a long docket, read the charges. "Evidence?"

Sergeant Bleyle stood. "Your Honor, a witness, Mr. Jacob a.k.a. 'Jake' Smith, saw the accused exit the room where the theft occurred. The room, the teachers' lounge, is strictly off-limits to students. No one except Mr. Smith, the principal, and the vice principal had access to the building after hours. Unfortunately, the theft wasn't discovered until early this morning."

The judge thought for a moment. "Amount of the theft?"

"Estimated at slightly over five dollars."

"Any priors?" he asked Bleyle, referring to Tom's arrest record.

"No, Your Honor."

"The defendant will approach the bench," Judge Clark ordered, beckoning Tom to the desk. "How do you plead, Mr. van Sloten?"

"I didn't do it, sir," he croaked, voice taut with strain.

"Son, it's customary to refer to me as 'Your Honor.' But 'sir' will do. Now, you have to answer whether you're guilty or not guilty."

"Not guilty, sir—I mean, Your Honor," Tom answered firmly as a ghost of a smile crossed the judge's face.

"Tom," Judge Clark reproved gently, "we give ourselves a lot of latitude in the way we handle first-time offenders. We're pretty informal here. The goal of this whole process is to see you don't get into trouble again. We don't want to throw the book at you, son. We won't if you come clean and make restitution. I think Sergeant Bleyle's already told you that you'll get off easier if you tell us the truth. Now, not later."

"I'm not guilty, Judge. I was somewhere I shouldn't have been. I admit that. But I didn't take the money! I *swear* I didn't!" Tom insisted.

Judge Clark shook his head with regret. "Tom, I think you need to stew about this for a while. Like over Christmas." He banged his gavel and intoned, "The accused is remanded to the custody of his parents. The formal hearing will be held Monday, January 15th."

Sergeant Bleyle spoke up, "What about bail, Your Honor?"

"Bail?" the judge queried with a knowing smile. "Bail is usually imposed to make sure the defendant will appear in court to answer to the legal process. We don't use bail in juvenile court, Sergeant. You know better than that," Judge Clark chided.

Bleyle shrugged.

"We release juveniles to the custody of their parents *if* the parents are reliable and *if* the juveniles pose no danger to the community. Otherwise they go to juvenile detention." The judge turned to Tom. "You're not going to skip out on us, are you, Tom?"

"Nossir. I mean no, Your Honor."

The judge glanced at Tom's parents. "Mr. and Mrs. van Sloten, is Tom responsive to your control and can you guarantee his appearance at court when ordered?"

"Yes, Your Honor," Hendrik mumbled.

"Your Honor," Bleyle argued. "Shoplifting and petty theft have more than doubled compared to last year. If we don't make an example of someone and nip this trend early, we're going to have an even bigger problem next year. Nits make lice, I always say."

"Your point's well taken," the judge conceded. "So I'm going to release Tom to *you*, Sergeant, for *your* determination of whether he should be released to his parents or sent to the detention center." He banged his gavel again. "Next case!"

Tom's shoulders sagged. If Bleyle wouldn't release him to his parents, it meant jail. Then he remembered what the sergeant had said earlier: "Five dollars. *Now!*" Bail or restitution, it didn't matter what they called it. If he couldn't come up with five dollars he would still go to jail.

It was jail or Christmas.

❧ CHAPTER EIGHTEEN ❧
Monday afternoon, December 18, 1933

Sergeant Bleyle waited while the van Slotens conferred in the hall outside the juvenile court. Tom was surprisingly calm. "Dad, I want you and Mom to go home. Look in the top dresser drawer on the sleeping porch. My money jar's hidden under some clothes at the back. There's a bit more than five dollars in it. Please bring it back and get me out of here!"

"We have to keep Tom here until you can post restitution for him, Mr. van Sloten. Real sorry, but that's the way it has to be," Bleyle apologized as he ushered Tom to the court's holding area.

The forbidding room with its barred doors and windows was filled with an odd assortment of vagrants and petty criminals, rough-looking characters who gave Tom the creeps. One of them snarled at him, "Wha'cha lookin' at, kid?"

"N—nothing," he stuttered. Chastened, he dropped his eyes and stared at the floor.

"That's better! Now keep it that way!"

"Aw, give him a break, Duke! He don't mean no harm," another tough put in. "Can't ya see the poor kid's scared half ta death?"

"Kid's got no manners," Tom's tormentor muttered as he spat on the floor in disgust.

Tom didn't dare look up. He glanced sideways at a policeman who was sitting near the door, feet propped up on a scarred desk. The officer ignored his silent plea for protection.

Tom tried to swallow, but his tongue stuck to the roof of his mouth. Without thinking, he stood up and walked to the door.

"Hey!" the policeman exclaimed, suddenly alert. "Where do you think *you're* goin'?"

"To—to get a drink of water. I'm thirsty," Tom stammered, thick-tongued.

"He's thirsty!" one of the prisoners mocked. They all laughed.

"Sit down!" the policeman ordered. "You ain't goin' nowhere, kid! You don't move a muscle 'less I say you can."

Tom sat, cowed into miserable silence. As the minutes crept by, all he could think about was his dumb mistake in the teachers' lounge. It had seemed like such a little thing at the time. Now it loomed as an innocent but terrible error that threatened to wreck everything.

It was an eternity before Hendrik returned, clutching the jar. He surrendered the five dollars, signed the necessary papers, and took custody of his son.

Weak with relief, Tom took a deep breath as they left the City and County Building. "I just learned something important," he exhaled as he faced his father. "About freedom. You never know what it means until you don't have it. I couldn't even get a drink of water in there without getting permission."

He couldn't bear to look at the empty jar.

The American History class was busy looking up answers to the questions Hazel Whitcomb had passed out when Tom slipped into the room. He slumped at his desk, staring sightlessly out the window.

"Tom!" Hazel reproved gently, "are you all right? You look as if your mind is a million miles away."

"Sorry, Mrs. Whitcomb. I guess it is."

"I need to see you after school. You, too," she said, pointing at Eliza. "Sorry I missed you last Friday. I was, shall we say, 'shanghaied' after class. It won't take long."

"Eliza. Tom. Come in," Mrs. Whitcomb invited. "Have a seat. I want to show you something I think might interest both of you." She handed each student a crisp brochure. "This is the new scholarship I mentioned to you on the phone, Tom. It's a merit scholarship the Utah Historical Society is sponsoring to encourage interest in history. Each high school in the state is allowed to nominate two students. I've suggested to Dr. Schneider we should nominate both of you."

The two rivals eyed each other.

"The award is based on academic record, letters of recommendation, scholarship, and citizenship. East will supply a copy of your grades. You'll need at least two letters, one of which is supposed to come from a history teacher—I'll be glad to write them—and the other from the principal. Dr.

Schneider was quite excited when I told him about the new scholarship last week. He thinks you would be very competitive candidates and plans to write a strong letter for each of you. We want East to have the first winner."

Tom wasn't sure Dr. Schneider would be so enthusiastic.

"Scholarship means demonstrating the ability to think creatively, do research, and write a cogent essay delineating a topic of your choosing. Submitting an essay is part of the application." Mrs. Whitcomb stopped as Eliza rolled her eyes. "You can use the next semester's term paper as your essay, Eliza. It won't be extra work. The only problem *you* might have is your tendency to procrastinate. The applications—*with* the essay—are due April 15th. The term paper won't be due until the last week of school."

Mrs. Whitcomb handed a packet of materials to each student. "The last part, citizenship, is more subjective. The committee in charge of drawing up criteria for the scholarship insisted each applicant must be of 'outstanding character.' They debated what that meant and how it could be demonstrated. They finally decided each applicant must have a letter from the Dean of Boys or Girls attesting to their good citizenship."

Tom groaned inwardly. A sly smile crept across Eliza's face.

"Any questions?" Mrs. Whitcomb asked. Both Eliza and Tom shook their heads. "It's a wonderful opportunity," she concluded. "You'll be interested to see that the scholarship includes tuition, fees, and a small stipend for books and supplies. Quite a handsome award, I think. In addition to the honor, of course."

"Mrs. Whitcomb, could I see you a moment? Alone?" Tom hesitated, glancing at Eliza.

"Of course. Eliza, if you'll excuse us."

Eliza shrugged as she left the room.

Tom turned to face his teacher. "Mrs. Whitcomb, I'm afraid I may not be eligible for the scholarship."

Hazel was dumbfounded. "For heaven's sake! Why not? You're the ideal candidate, Tom."

Tom hung his head. "Citizenship. I don't think the Historical Society would choose someone with a criminal record."

"*You* have a criminal record, Tom? I don't believe it!"

"As of today, I do."

Tom told her the whole story. "I didn't do it, Mrs. Whitcomb. I just don't know how I can prove it."

"*I* believe you, Tom. Furthermore, you're innocent until proven guilty."

"What am I going to do, Mrs. Whitcomb? We can't afford a lawyer."

"I don't know, Tom," she answered honestly. "I suppose the court will appoint one for you. But this whole thing seems too—well, *pat*. Something is missing here, and it isn't just the money!"

❧ CHAPTER NINETEEN ❧

Monday afternoon, December 18, 1933

Hazel switched off the lights in her classroom and closed the door. The hallways were deserted, already darkening as the late afternoon faded in the short December day. On a hunch, she walked to Jim Siddons's classroom. He was still at his desk, grading papers. Jim looked weary, his drawn face set in a grim smile.

"You've heard?" he asked without preamble.

Hazel nodded.

"Hazel, I just can't get it out of my mind. The sight of a policeman hauling Tom van Sloten out of Schneider's office. The poor kid looked poleaxed. Then there was Garrison, standing there with that infuriating smirk. He didn't have to say 'I told you so'; it was written all over his face."

Siddons grimaced. "The heck of it is, it's partly my fault. I hate to admit it, but Garrison was right. We shouldn't have left all that money lying around. If I'd just—"

"No, Jim. It wasn't you that took the money. *That's* the crime, not your failure to follow Garrison's orders."

"Do you think Tom really did it?"

Hazel shook her head emphatically. "Absolutely not. He talked to me, told me the whole story. He says he didn't take the money."

"You believe him?"

"Yes I do. I think Tom's telling the truth."

"Me too. Tell you what, Hazel. Friend of mine is a sergeant on the police force. I'll give him a call and see what he can find out. If I learn anything, I'll call you at home tonight."

Tom sat on his bunk bed, head buried in his hands. The empty glass jar lay on its side, the remaining few coins scattered on the blanket. They mocked his pathetic attempt at substituting for Santa.

No money for Christmas dinner. No more gifts.

The vision of Santa Claus in handcuffs or behind bars haunted him.

He walked to the dresser and reluctantly opened his drawer, removing the velvet box. The golden eagle glowed in the twilight. He caressed it for the last time, then shoved the box into his pants and walked downtown.

Delaney's Coin Shop was still open.

"Mr. Delaney? Remember me? The kid with the double eagle gold piece?"

Delaney looked up, surprised. "I—sure! Tom van Sloten. Haven't seen you for a few years. My gosh, you've grown up!"

Tom pulled the box out of his pocket. "How much is this worth now, Mr. Delaney?"

Delaney put a jeweler's loupe in his eye and squinted at the coin, scrutinizing both sides. "Perfect," he pronounced. He looked up at Tom. "Some of these double eagles are still circulating. Most are worth just their face value. Five dollars. But yours is in mint condition. That might add a dollar or two."

Tom's eyes widened. "I need to sell it. Now. Are you still interested?"

"Tom," Delaney replied as he removed the loupe, "this is a bad time to sell coins. Lots of people are doing it, and it's driven the prices down. I know six or seven dollars sounds like a fortune. But it's a fraction of what the double eagle will be worth in a few years. You hold on to it and you won't be sorry, I promise you."

"I can't, Mr. Delaney. I really need the money now. Not ten years from now."

"Young fella like you—what's the big rush? It's not like you're married with a bunch of kids. You've got all the time in the world."

"I've got exactly six days, Mr. Delaney. Six days till Christmas. I *had* the money. Until this morning, that is. Then—well, never mind. I don't have it now. Will you buy the double eagle? If you won't, I'll have to go somewhere else."

"You're making a mistake, Tom. Keep the coin. Trust me. Someday you'll be glad you did."

Tom was adamant. "Do you want it or not, Mr. Delaney?"

Delaney shook his head as he unlocked the cash register. "Oh, I want it all right. Any dealer would. But I'm telling you—" He stopped at the determined look on Tom's face.

Delaney filled out an invoice documenting the coin's price and provenance. Then he pulled out a brand-new five dollar bill and handed it to Tom.

"But you said six or seven—"

"Read the invoice, son."

"12/18/33. Received from Thomas van Sloten, esq. One 1908 double eagle gold piece. Condition: uncirculated. Face value: five dollars. Will be held by Delaney Coins, Inc., in perpetuity for said Thomas van Sloten and may be repurchased at any time for face value."

Tom looked up, a glimmer of hope dawning. "Does this mean . . . ?"

"Yep," Delaney replied, looking pleased with himself. "Five bucks will get you the double eagle back, any time. Now or forever. Tell me—" he hesitated, "is five dollars enough?"

Tom grinned. "Mr. Delaney, it's exactly enough!"

Hazel Whitcomb curled up in her favorite chair, her beloved golden retriever, Sticks, at her feet. A cheery fire blazed away in the wide brick fireplace. Sticks shoved his nose under her hand, begging for attention. Absently, she stroked the dog's head as he grunted with pleasure.

The phone rang, breaking the stillness.

"Hazel? Jim here. I talked with my friend downtown. Sergeant Bleyle. 'Fraid I've got bad news."

Hazel caught her breath.

"Tom stole the money. No doubt about it. They've got him dead to rights. His fingerprints were all over the mug."

T he last days before Christmas passed in a blur. Tom felt like a zombie, the walking dead shunned by live, flesh-and-blood people. His classmates seemed to avoid meeting his gaze, glancing at him sideways and sliding their eyes away before he could respond. Even Louie Chaffos and Dean Lindsay gave him a wide berth. Tom wanted to yell, *I don't have the bubonic plague! I'm alive! Look at me, for gosh sake!*

Jeannie treated him as if he had already been tried, convicted, and sentenced. Once he thought he heard her whisper behind her hand to a friend nearby, "Saint Tom's fallen off his pedestal!"

He became an unwitting member of a group that he didn't want to join. The day after his arrest, the East High Outlaws adopted him as one of their own.

"Tom! Hey, Tom!" One of the Outlaws came up to him in the hall and punched him playfully in the shoulder. "I hear you're one of us now. Even got yourself a 'sheet' down in Juvie. Way to go!"

Tom winced, and not from the punch.

The only good news during the whole miserable week was that business picked up at Rosenblatt's Department Store. Now payday would add another dollar or two to the five he had received from Mr. Delaney. He still needed to buy Jean's gift and the stuff for Christmas dinner. That would leave around a dollar for contingencies. If there were no more emergencies, it would start the college fund all over again.

Tom tried to observe what was fashionable with teenage girls. He wandered through the women's department at Rosenblatt's and even glanced at a few fashion magazines the store always kept on hand. It made him feel silly, but he did it anyway. He looked at the price tags on a few items and blanched. Everything was too expensive.

"Hey, Tom!" The stockroom door flew open as his supervisor stuck his head around the corner. "The boss wants t'see ya."

"Me?" Tom asked, incredulous.

"Yeah, you! Yer the only Tom workin' here, ain't ya?"

"Guess so," Tom admitted. His stomach lurched. Maybe Mr. Rosenblatt didn't want an employee with a 'sheet,' as the Outlaws called the criminal record. If he lost his job right before Christmas, it would be a disaster.

"Well, whatcha waitin' for?" the supervisor asked. "Don't keep the boss waitin'!"

Tom hurried to the elevator, riding it upstairs to the office complex. He had never been in what the employees called "The Throne Room."

He entered the reception area, heart pounding with apprehension.

A handsome, smartly dressed older woman was sitting in the waiting room, thumbing through a glossy fashion magazine. She looked at him for a moment before she returned to her reading. Tom smiled weakly and turned toward the receptionist. She was engrossed in her typing, fingernails clacking a rhythmic tattoo on the metal keys.

He cleared his throat. His mouth was so dry he could hardly talk. "Excuse me," he asked deferentially. "I'm Tom van Sloten. I think Mr. Rosenblatt wanted to see me."

"Oh. Tom. Yes, he's expecting you. Door's open so you can go right in."

Nerves jangling, Tom took a deep breath. He offered a silent prayer as he stepped into the office.

Mr. Rosenblatt was seated behind the largest desk Tom had ever seen, working in rolled-up shirtsleeves with his collar loosened and tie askew. He was shuffling through papers and dictating letters rapid-fire to a secretary who was scribbling shorthand as fast as she could write. Three—*three!*—telephones perched on a credenza at a right angle to the enormous desk.

Tom couldn't imagine what such a busy man would want with an unimportant employee like him.

"You wanted to see me, sir?"

"Tom van Sloten. Yes, I did. Anita, if you'd excuse us just a minute . . . And please ask Stella to hold my calls, too."

The secretary closed her steno pad and exited gracefully, swinging the door shut with a barely perceptible click.

They were alone. Mr. Rosenblatt looked at Tom with total concentration, papers and telephones forgotten. "Please sit down," he said, gesturing toward the vacated chair near his desk. "Make yourself comfortable."

Make myself comfortable? Tom wondered, scarcely daring to hope. Those didn't sound like the words of someone who was about to fire an employee.

Mr. Rosenblatt looked at him for a moment, saying nothing. Tom had the uncanny sensation that those piercing blue eyes were peering into his very soul. Finally he spoke. "One of your teachers, Hazel Whitcomb, is a good customer and close friend of ours."

Tom held his breath. To his surprise, Mr. Rosenblatt smiled. "Hazel tells me you're the brightest student she's ever had. Said she gave you what she called 'full marks' on your American History term paper. If East High allowed an A+, which I gather they don't, she would have given you one of those. Says she's never done that before, but your essay was a brilliant piece of work and deserved it.

"You're a hard worker, Tom," Mr. Rosenblatt continued. "I've heard good things about you from the people here in the store. Hazel also told us a bit about your family. I gather your parents have had some struggles. Hazel says you're trying to save enough to attend the university this fall."

"Yessir," Tom nodded, trying hard not to think about his demolished savings and the hocked coin.

Mr. Rosenblatt leaned back in his chair as a dreamy look stole across his face. "Let me tell you a little story," he reminisced. "My father, Nathan Rosenblatt, grew up in Czarist Russia. In those days the vast majority of Russian Jews were kept within severely restricted areas. They couldn't live or work outside these enclaves. They couldn't move without written permission. They were forbidden to own land. They were prohibited from practicing most crafts, skills, and trades. With rare exceptions, they weren't allowed to attend colleges or universities.

"The Rosenblatts lived in a *shtetl*, a small Jewish village near Brest-Litovsk. The living conditions in such places were dreadful. Around 1880, when Nathan was just about your age, the pogroms began again. Troops of cossacks roamed the countryside, pillaging and burning one *shtetl* after another. They beat our people without mercy, torturing and killing some, doing unspeakable things to others. As always, the police looked the other way. The outrages were ignored. No one was safe, not even the women and children. The Jews were defenseless.

"The last straw came when the Russian Army started to conscript young boys—just children, really. One night my grandfather called Nathan, his oldest son, to his side. He gave him a rail ticket to Hamburg, Germany, and a small purse filled with coins. He said, 'Pack. You're leaving tonight. This is everything we have. Go to America.' My father, startled and afraid, began to protest. 'Go to America,' my grandfather repeated. Then he said, 'I don't know what will happen to you there. But I do know what will happen to you here.'"

Mr. Rosenblatt paused, overcome with emotion. "So my father left. Like lots of immigrants from Poland and Russia, he never saw his family again. He made his way across Europe and then worked for his transatlantic passage on a freighter bound for New York. When he arrived, he knew no one. Not a single soul. He spoke only Russian and Yiddish. Our people tried to help him, but times were tough then, not so different from now.

"Dad's parents had friends who had ended up in Colorado. Told there might be more opportunities in the West, he left Brooklyn and hopped a freight train to Denver. When he got there he found the people so destitute that they barely had enough to feed their own family. He couldn't find a job, so eventually he came here. He started with a pushcart and went door to door, selling dry goods on consignment for the Auerbach brothers."

Tom was fascinated. "And I thought *we* had it hard," he murmured.

"People liked and trusted Dad," Mr. Rosenblatt continued. "He had a real knack for business. He worked hard, learning English until he could speak without an accent. He saved as much as he could and eventually started his own company selling parts and supplies to mining camps. That's how all this started," Mr. Rosenblatt gestured. Then he apologized. "Forgive an old man for rambling on and on. You're an indulgent listener."

Tom started to protest, "I'm not—"

Mr. Rosenblatt held up his hand, stopping Tom in midsentence. "Yes, Tom, you are. Mrs. Whitcomb says you pay close attention and never forget anything. She says you're a voracious reader as well."

Suddenly he smacked his head in mock dismay. "Cut to the point, Rosenblatt!" he chided himself out loud. "I'm taking too much of your time. Two things. First, if you ever need help with college, come talk to me. Somehow I feel you won't. You have a lot of pride, I think. But I'll be here just in case. Second thing," he continued as he reached into his desk and pulled out an envelope. "The full-time employees here receive a holiday bonus. That's not been the case for the part-timers and temporary help. I'm going to make an exception."

He pushed the envelope toward Tom. "Go ahead, son," he urged. "Open it."

It was a five-dollar gift certificate, good at any Rosenblatt store.

Tom was astonished. "Mr. Rosenblatt, I didn't earn this. I—I can't accept it," he stammered.

"You for doggone sure can!" Mr. Rosenblatt insisted. "Now, if you prefer cash instead, you can turn in the certificate at the cashier's office on the second floor. If you choose to use the certificate, you'll also get the full employee discount on any items you purchase here. That's 20 percent, by the way."

Tom hesitated. Unbidden, the double eagle flashed into his mind. He could take the five dollars and retrieve his treasure from Mr. Delaney.

"Thanks, Mr. Rosenblatt. I'd like to use the certificate here," he decided, pushing the thought of the coin firmly out of his consciousness. "I need to find something for my sister, Jeannie."

Mr. Rosenblatt didn't seem surprised. "Good!" he exclaimed. "Now let's go find Mrs. Rosenblatt."

"*Mrs.* Rosenblatt?"

"Yes, Mrs. Rosenblatt. My wife, Evelyn. My 'informants' tell me you're not very experienced in picking out women's things. Mrs. Rosenblatt is a real expert," he said, winking as he pushed the button to his intercom.

"Stella, would you please ask Evelyn to come in here for a moment?" The door opened, and the handsome older woman Tom had noticed earlier entered with a broad smile.

"Evelyn, this is young Tom van Sloten, Hazel's top student. Tom, meet Mrs. Rosenblatt. She's the brains behind this particular operation! Evelyn helps buy all the women's fashions each season. You won't go wrong following her advice. She has a few minutes before we go out to dinner at 6:00. Take advantage of it!"

Tom shook Mrs. Rosenblatt's hand with a questioning look.

"Let's get started," she ordered as she took the gift certificate from his hand and examined it with approval. "Five dollars. That should do the job!"

She turned on her heels, gesturing for Tom to follow. "Thank you, sir!" he blurted as Mr. Rosenblatt waved him off and turned back to his desk.

Mrs. Rosenblatt marched Tom to the women's specialty department. The clerks greeted her with deference.

"How old is your sister?" Mrs. Rosenblatt inquired.

"Fourteen. Almost fifteen," he corrected himself as he wondered, *How does she know I have a sister?*

"Size?"

Tom blushed. "I—I'm not sure," he replied, flustered.

"About like me?"

"More like that lady," Tom said, pointing shyly to one of the hovering clerks.

"Size eight," Mrs. Rosenblatt pronounced with authority. "Now, in her heart of hearts just about every girl wants one of these new sweater 'twin sets.' Like this one," she said, pointing to a soft-looking cardigan in a handsome display case. It was artfully arranged, opened just enough to show off the matching short-sleeved sweater underneath. A single strand of pearls draped at the neck completed the stylish effect.

The outfit was beautiful. Tom knew Jean would be thrilled.

"What sort of coloring does she have?" Mrs. Rosenblatt asked. "Like you? Dark hair? Brown eyes? Fair skin?"

Tom nodded.

"Then this isn't the right color," she decided. "Danielle, what other colors do we have in a size eight?"

The clerk opened a drawer behind the counter and removed several different possibilities.

"Black. Nice when she's fifty. Not fifteen," Mrs. Rosenblatt judged. "Mint green. Not bad. This pale blue would be nice too."

The last set in the stack was a soft peach color. Tom took one look at it and knew it was right. "That one. That one would be just perfect."

"You have excellent taste, young man," Mrs. Rosenblatt complimented him. Then, much to his embarrassment, she held the sweater next to his face. "Look in the mirror," she ordered. "You wouldn't wear this color yourself, of course, but it will look fabulous on your sister."

"How much is it?" Tom knew it wouldn't be cheap.

Danielle turned the tag over. "Four-fifty," she read. "With the employee discount that would be three dollars and sixty cents."

"Make it an even three-fifty," Mrs. Rosenblatt instructed.

A king's—or a queen's—ransom. Tom guessed his mother had never paid that much for a sweater in her entire life.

"I'll take it," he declared.

"Excellent. Danielle will gift wrap that for you while we finish up," Mrs. Rosenblatt said, glancing at her slim diamond wristwatch.

Finish up? Tom glanced at her, raising his eyebrows.

"Your parents," she reminded him. "They're the only ones left, aren't they?"

Where does this astonishing woman get her information? he marveled. With Jean's gift, the official "Santa list" was finished. But it *would* be a wonderful surprise to get something for Mom and Dad, even if it were a modest present. He could give it to them on behalf of all the children.

"Your mother could use a warm scarf and matching gloves, I think," she said, eyes twinkling. "We can find something appropriate for your father, too."

She whisked him off to the accessories department. "Kid gloves aren't very practical. Not warm enough. But these cotton chamoisuede ones are washable. Wool would also be nice," she mused, pointing to an array of scarves and gloves in bright colors.

Tom was losing his reticence. He looked at the price. One-fifty.

"Make that a dollar," Mrs. Rosenblatt directed the clerk.

Tom chose a bright red set. "I think she'll like these," he said with growing confidence.

"Now for your father." Mrs. Rosenblatt headed toward the department labeled *Men's Furnishings*. "He has a fine voice. I've heard him perform. He sings Harry Lauder's Scottish songs better than Harry Lauder himself!"

Tom was beyond amazement. "Dad does perform quite a bit," he admitted.

"Does he have a tartan tie?"

"I don't think so," Tom answered, struggling to picture his father's scanty wardrobe.

"Then he should have one for his performances. There are some very nice ties here we can let you have for fifty cents," she smiled, guessing Tom's thoughts as he mentally totaled the purchases. That would make exactly five dollars.

Tom spotted a handsome one, a Royal Stuart tartan. Perfect.

He was done.

"Six o'clock, Mr. Rosenblatt," Stella announced as she bustled into the office. "You go ahead. I'll lock up." She helped him into his topcoat, handing him his hat and muffler as he slipped on his gloves.

"I'll do it, Stella. Please go downstairs and tell Evelyn I'll be along in a minute or two."

Mr. Rosenblatt straightened the papers on his desk and rounded the office, turning off lights and closing up for the night. He headed for the door, then changed his mind and walked to the large window that overlooked Main Street. To the east, the snow-covered Wasatch Mountains shimmered in the early moonrise. He never tired of the spectacular sight. As he gazed down, he saw Tom leave the store laden with packages. The boy waved to someone and then sprinted down the street.

"*Mazel tov*, young Tom van Sloten," he murmured as he watched the tall figure disappear into the night. Then he smiled and whispered, "And Merry Christmas, too."

❧ CHAPTER TWENTY-ONE ❧
Saturday, December 23, 1933

Tom worked at a furious pace, completing all the restocking at Rosenblatt's by noon. Mrs. Rosenblatt insisted on having the full panoply of merchandise on display for the last-minute shoppers who seemed to materialize out of nowhere. To accommodate their best customers and most demanding clientele, the store would close at 6:00 P.M. and then reopen for private shopping and a special holiday reception that lasted until 9:00 in the evening.

Tom ran to Eldridge's cycle shop. The now-familiar jingle of the doorbell greeted him as he burst into the store. Mr. Eldridge was assisting two last-minute shoppers, a well-dressed couple who were having a spirited argument about which shiny new bicycle to buy their youngest boy. The Elgin Redbird would be just fine, the man insisted in a loud voice, pointing to the least expensive variety. No, his wife countered, equally vehement, he should have the top-of-the-line Black Hawk. Fully chrome-plated, at $34.95 it was almost twice as expensive as the Redbird.

Tom waited, shifting his weight from one foot to the other, trying to be patient. The couple finally compromised on a blue Falcon with a bold red stripe on its fenders. With a resigned air, the man pulled three crisp ten-dollar bills from his wallet and pushed them across the counter. Mumbling to himself, he wheeled the new bicycle through the door and loaded it into the trunk of their sedan. Tom could see the two of them still gesticulating at each other as they drove off.

Mr. Eldridge shook his head at the departing car. "Believe it or not, Tom, there *is* such a thing as having too much," he remarked.

Tom couldn't imagine it. "Is the bike finished, Mr. Eldridge?"

"Sure is. And it looks terrific, if I may say so myself," he grinned. "I'll get it for you."

Mr. Eldridge emerged a moment later from the back room pushing the bicycle. "Well," he asked with pride, "what do you think?"

Tom stared at it, rubbing his eyes in disbelief. There had to be a mistake. This wasn't his bicycle; it was a brand-new one!

"Mr. Eldridge, I can't afford a new one. Where's my old one?" he asked, panic edging his voice.

"This *is* your old one!" Mr. Eldridge exclaimed. "Lookit. We took the dents out of the fenders and repainted them. Got new rubber grips on the handlebars and put a brand-new leather seat on the frame. Polished and oiled all the spokes and sprockets till there wasn't a single speck of rust left! The tires and pedals were still in good shape, so we just applied this special black goop we got. Then rubbed 'em real good. Made 'em look just like new! We even put on a new basket so's Richard'll have a place for his books."

Tom squatted down and peered at the bicycle. Sure enough, it was his. But Mr. Eldridge and his son had done such a masterful restoration that it looked brand-new.

He smiled in relief, knowing that Richard would never guess their secret. "Thanks, Mr. Eldridge. You sure had me fooled. It looks just great!

Richard won't believe his eyes. I'll give you the eight hours starting right after Christmas."

He hid the bicycle along with the other Santa gifts in their neighbor's garage and headed home, bursting with contentment. *It's done*, he thought with deep satisfaction.

Santa was ready.

The van Sloten house vibrated with activity. Tom's mouth watered at the rich, tantalizing odor of freshly baked cookies. "Any broken ones?" he asked, spying his favorite Scottish shortbreads. Requiring a full pound of butter, they were a rare treat his mother reserved for the holidays.

"No," Sarah winked, "but you deserve a whole one. Just one, now, mind you!" she admonished as he ate one of the delicious confections, taking small bites to make the taste last as long as possible.

"Dad home?"

"In the bedroom. He's wrapping some things for tomorrow night."

Tom knew from experience what 'things' meant. It was always new pajamas they would all unwrap on Christmas Eve. *Necessities made into gifts*, he thought sadly.

Jean entered the kitchen, squeezing water from a pair of soapy socks.

"Hey, Tom!" she greeted her brother. "I'm washing out my gym socks. This year I'm going to hang up a really *big* stocking!"

Stocking? Tom was confused. Then he gasped in dismay. Stockings!

Oh no, he thought in mounting horror. *I forgot the stockings!*

He had no time! The sun, describing a low arc across the late December sky, was already setting behind the Oquirrh Mountains far to the west. Tom grabbed his jacket and dumped the last few coins from the glass jar into his pockets. He dashed out the door and sprinted all the way downtown, reaching the Salt Lake 5 & 10 Cent Store as the last remnants of daylight faded from the sky.

Only twenty minutes remained until the store closed for the weekend. The employees, eager to leave for the holiday, were already shepherding the last few customers toward the doors.

Tom hurried down the nearest aisle, frantically scanning the shelves for stocking stuffers. He quickly found two tiny matchbox cars and plunked down two dimes. That took care of Paul and Davey. The clerk wrote up the bill, placing it and Tom's money in a metal container that she pulled along wires in the ceiling to the central cashier on the second floor. The change came back in the cylinder. The two cents hardly seemed worth the wait.

He ran down another aisle and picked up several colored drawing pencils. Two for a nickel! Richard was a good artist and loved to sketch. *He'll like these*, Tom concluded as he gave the clerk the exact change and pocketed the pencils.

That left Jeannie. Always Jeannie! Girls could be such a pain, he thought in annoyance. He spied a counter with a sign, "Costume Jewelry." That was it. A necklace. A pin. Something that would complement the sweater set. Earrings and a strand of artificial pearls looked appealing, but at a dollar twenty-nine they were far over budget. He pulled an imitation gold-and-pearl butterfly pin from a revolving display. Not bad. It would have to do.

How can I fill the rest of the stockings? he wondered, recalling Jean's remarks and her oversized sock. *Something that takes up a lot of room and still doesn't cost too much.*

"Candy!" he exclaimed out loud, startling another shopper.

Perspiring with effort, he rushed to the candy counter. "Half pound of those giant gumdrops, please! Another half pound of the hard candies! And four—make that five—chocolate Santas!" he ordered the bemused clerk. The closing chimes sounded as she weighed the last bag and rang up the total.

"That'll be twenty-five cents, please."

Tom sighed as he counted out the exact change. *I guess that's what contingency funds are for. The unexpected. Or, in this case, the overlooked.*

He was the last one to leave the store. He peeked in his sack, noticing it didn't look very full. His last-minute purchases wouldn't come close to filling the stockings. They'd be half-empty. He was sure they'd look forlorn, unfinished.

Exhausted, Tom trudged toward home.

Hales' Market, the mom-and-pop grocery store around the block from their house, was still open. Mr. Hales was a grumpy, buck-toothed old man with a famously short temper. His wife, a domineering and irascible woman, had a large wart on her nose that had a long black hair growing out of it. Some of the neighborhood children whispered that she was a witch. With the mindless cruelty of the young, they sometimes double-dared each other to run up and touch her. Tom had never taunted the old woman, but he still hated to go in there. Especially now. He knew his parents still owed the Hales for last week's groceries. *But it's worth a try*, he thought, ancient fear souring his stomach.

He was relieved that Mrs. Hales wasn't in the store. Mr. Hales lurked behind the counter, a soiled apron knotted around his protruding middle. "Sarah send you out to do a little last-minute shopping?" he scowled, implying *and I suppose she wants it on credit, too*.

"No sir, not at all. I think she's got everything she needs already," Tom answered, ashamed that he couldn't keep a childish quaver out of his voice.

"So what's all the rush about?"

"I'm doing the kids' stockings this year, Mr. Hales. The problem is, I'm fresh out of ideas and almost out of money," Tom confessed. "What can you suggest for," he paused, counting out his remaining coins, "twenty-eight cents? It can't be very much."

Mr. Hales stared at him, shaking his head. "Twenty-eight cents? That's a *lot* of money! In my day, sonny . . . Well," he grumbled, "forget my day. This is *today*. Modern times, I say.

"Start with a real treat," he prescribed as he shuffled to the fruit bins. "Oranges. Two for a nickel. I bring 'em in special, just for Christmas."

Of course. Tom had forgotten the much-anticipated treat and how much fun it was to peel back the fragrant rind, exposing the plump, juicy segments . . . pop one into your mouth and bite down. Let the tangy juice run down your throat in a sweet-tart stream. He licked his lips at the memory. Oranges would fill the toes of the stocking nicely, too.

"Nuts. Lots of nuts," Mr. Hales continued, a sudden whirlwind of activity. He scooped a generous amount of mixed Brazil nuts, pecans, walnuts, and hazelnuts into a paper bag without weighing it. "Keeps the kids occupied, cracking these things. Lotta work, small reward. But hey, trust me! They love it! Sit in front of the fire . . . yeah. That's *fun!*

"Marshmallow snowmen," he insisted. "Can't stand 'em myself. Too sweet and gooey. Day after Christmas I couldn't give these things away. Might as well let you have 'em now. Compliments of the house." He shot Tom a toothy grin.

"Last but not least, you need something really special to go right on top. Stick out of the stocking. There's a real art to this stuff, you know," he concluded as he selected some giant peppermint candy canes.

"Twenty-eight cents exactly," Mr. Hales proclaimed, ringing the amount into the cash register.

Tom was too numb with fatigue to argue. "Thanks, Mr. Hales! And a Merry Christmas to you and Mrs. Hales, too. I won't forget this," he promised as he left the store, banging the door shut.

♣ CHAPTER TWENTY-TWO ♣
Saturday evening, December 23, 1933

R osenblatt's Department Store reopened after regular hours for the traditional holiday reception to which the most favored customers were invited. Soft music filtered through the store as elegantly dressed clients—mostly men—shopped for a few last-minute items. Waiters circulated with trays of hot and cold hors d'oeuvres. Guests could choose between tall fluted glasses of champagne—domestic this year, not imported French—and cups of nonalcoholic fruit punch. Joe and Evelyn mingled with the customers, greeting friends and offering helpful advice on purchases.

This year the reception was even more crowded than normal. As the Depression ground on and the financial uncertainties increased, the number of fancy Christmas parties in Federal Heights and the Avenues decreased. Though they wouldn't admit it, many of the customers were secretly relieved to enjoy someone else's largesse. A few of the more observant clients noticed that this year the Rosenblatts' hors d'oeuvres were somewhat less lavish than usual. A slightly worn collar here, a frayed cuff there betrayed the hard times.

The special pre-Christmas evening was Major Garrison's favorite time to shop for his Scandinavian-born wife. Each year his gift was the same: a personally selected nightgown and peignoir from Rosenblatt's.

The saleslady giggled as Garrison dangled a lovely silk nightgown from its thin shoulder straps. He let the material slide through his fingers, relishing the luxurious sensation. "What do you think about this one, Evelyn?" he inquired, wanting to confirm his choice.

"It's gorgeous, Major. Solvig will be delighted. You have such wonderful taste. She's a lucky woman."

Garrison raised his champagne glass. "So she is, Evelyn, so she is. But of course that makes me a lucky man!"

He turned to examine other possibilities, picking up a sheer black peignoir edged with fine lace and holding it up to his chest. He cocked an eyebrow at the saleslady. "You are a naughty, naughty boy, Mr. Garrison!" she tittered. "Are you buying that for yourself or Mrs. Garrison?" They both laughed.

An audible murmur suddenly filled the store. Garrison saw a few of the male customers move toward the broad, curved staircase that led up to the second-floor salon and dressing rooms. A tall blonde girl in a red taffeta dress was gliding down the steps. The fabric swished as she sashayed like a fashion model. A few of the men actually clapped in appreciation.

It was Eliza Cannon. Three of her girlfriends were standing at the bottom of the stairs. They looked green with envy.

"Eliza, you look positively *smashing!*"

"Bill Richards will just *die* when he sees you!"

"You'll be the life of the New Year's Eve party, for sure!"

Eliza smiled, basking in their admiration and enjoying their envy.

"Daddy usually comes tonight," she explained airily. "It's when he buys most of our presents. This year I guess the law practice isn't doing too well or something like that. He told me I couldn't have a new dress. So I decided to buy it myself!"

She pirouetted in front of the girls as the taffeta swished and crackled with static electricity. "What do you think? This one or the green velvet sheath?"

"The green looks great with your eyes," one of the girls flattered.

"I don't know, I sort of like the red," Eliza mused. She examined herself in the full-length mirror, slowly running her hands over her hips. "I think Bill would like this one. It feels so *sexy!*"

"Eliza!" The girls pretended shock.

"Maybe," she said, suddenly daring, "maybe what I ought to do is buy *both* dresses!"

"*Eliza!*" Now the girls were truly shocked. "Can you afford *two* dresses?"

"Not really," she admitted. "I just wanted to watch you all react. It's going to take all my savings to buy one dress. Decisions, decisions." She flounced back up the stairs.

Major Garrison had worked his way through most of the lingerie rack when Eliza reappeared, a dress in each hand. "I'm taking the green velvet," she announced. "We don't want to tempt Bill *too* much, now, do we?"

She handed the elegant dress to the saleslady. "This one, please." She put her purse on the countertop and turned it upside down. A pile of coins rattled onto the glass. At the sound Garrison edged closer, hidden behind the large Christmas tree next to the stairs.

The saleslady's fingers flew as she sorted the cash. Garrison saw her stop and point out several items in the pile. He watched as Eliza peered at them and laughed nervously, making light of it as she slipped the strange objects into her purse.

Garrison moved in, standing behind her.

"Good evening, Eliza! What a pleasant surprise to see you here," he murmured in her ear.

Eliza whirled at the familiar voice.

"M—Major Garrison! I mean Dean Garrison. Sir. It's, ah, n—nice to see you too," she stuttered.

"The girls are right. You did look very nice in that dress. Myself, I'd vote for the red," he added urbanely.

Eliza didn't know whether or not he was serious.

"I do hope you have a chance to wear it," Garrison said.

"Wha—what do you mean?" Eliza asked, suddenly wary.

"That's an interesting way you're paying for such an expensive dress, Eliza. All those loose coins and small bills. Most unusual, I'd say."

"Daddy said if I wanted a new dress I'd have to pay for it myself. So I—uh, I emptied my piggy bank," she added defensively.

"Aren't you a bit old for a 'piggy bank,' Eliza?"

"Aren't you a bit old to be pestering someone like me, Dean Garrison?" she retorted.

"Eliza," Garrison commanded, voice dangerously soft, "show me what you just put in your purse."

Her eyes widened in fear. "It's none of your business," she snapped. "A lady's purse is private."

"I think you're no lady, Eliza Gates Cannon. I can call store security and suggest I saw you shoplifting. They'll look in your purse and maybe some other places, too. Or you can show me. Your choice."

Eliza sniffled and let a tear trickle down her cheek.

Garrison was unmoved. "Crocodile tears. I've seen a lot of 'em. Won't work, Eliza. Not on me."

Defeated, Eliza reached into her purse and slowly pulled out three objects.

A British five-pence piece.

A New York City bus token.

And, last of all, a wooden nickel.

CHAPTER TWENTY-THREE
Saturday night, December 23, 1933

Tom stood at the living-room window, inhaling the Christmas smell of fresh pine and spices that filled the little house. Hendrik joined him, standing shoulder to shoulder in silent contemplation with his son.

"It's been a tough week, Tom," he sympathized.

Tom nodded, bone tired. "Yep. Sure has. I guess things'll never be the same. Not for anybody. After Christmas . . ."

"Don't think about that now, son. Things will—" Hendrik paused as a black car glided to a smooth stop in front of the house. Tom gaped. A tall figure in a long, belted coat, collar turned up, got out and walked up the sidewalk toward the house. A broad-brimmed fedora hid his features in deep shadow. Tom strained his eyes but couldn't identify the man. His heart fluttered wildly. Surely they wouldn't come for him this close to Christmas!

They heard the sound of heavy boots on the porch, then a soft but insistent rap on the front door.

Gulping, Tom turned the porch light on and opened the door. "Dean Garrison!" he gasped as the figure removed his hat. "Wh—why are you here?" Tom was immobile, frozen with fear.

"May I come in?"

"Of—of course," Tom blurted, turning to Hendrik in alarm. It was too late to flee.

"Come in, Mr. Garrison," Hendrik interceded in a polite but cautious voice. "Forgive my son. He forgot his manners. He didn't mean to be rude."

The three of them stood inside the door in an awkward knot, no one moving.

Sarah emerged from the kitchen. Her eyebrows flew up at the strange sight. She bustled toward the group, breaking the tense silence. "Well, don't everyone just stand there with the door open in this cold! Sit down. Let me take your coat, Mr. Garrison. I'll get us something to eat," she offered, wondering what she could sacrifice from the Christmas groceries for the unexpected visit.

Garrison waved her off. "Thank you, Mrs. van Sloten. You're too kind. That won't be necessary. This shouldn't take long." He sat on the sofa, hat in hand, and looked Tom squarely in the eyes.

"Tom, I owe you an apology. I—we—were too hasty. We jumped to the wrong conclusion. I've, uh, become aware of some new information that changes the whole unfortunate situation. You see, I was at Rosenblatt's tonight, shopping for Solvig . . ."

He told them the story.

"Eliza confessed?" Tom asked in wonder.

"To the whole thing. Seems her father's in a bit of a financial squeeze so he wouldn't—couldn't—buy her a new dress for some fancy New Year's Eve party she was going to attend with Bill Richards. She had her heart set on it. Last Friday she was looking for Hazel Whitcomb, just as you were. When she went into the teachers' lounge she saw the coffee money. *And* your note. She took both. Says she never intended for you to take the blame, but the whole thing snowballed out of control. She was too scared to tell the truth. I'm sure that when they look, the police will find her fingerprints on the mug too."

Garrison paused. "I might never have put two and two together without the wooden nickel, the New York City bus token, and the five-pence piece. The teachers had joked about putting those into the mug in lieu of cash."

"Poor Eliza," Tom empathized.

"*Poor Eliza my—!*" Garrison expostulated. "Forgive my outburst," he apologized. "She was going to let you take the rap, Tom. She doesn't deserve your sympathy. Eliza has to learn there are consequences to breaking the law and then lying about it."

He stood. "Never mind. We'll get everything straightened out after Christmas, believe me. I'll see to it myself. You have my word of honor on that."

Garrison clapped his fedora on his head and touched the brim. "Mr. van Sloten. Mrs. van Sloten. My regards. And Merry Christmas, too."

He headed out the door and down the steps. They heard the engine roar to life. Then he was gone.

The van Slotens heaved a huge sigh. Then they were shouting with relief, hugging and pounding each other on the back.

"Guess Santa's not goin' to jail after all!" Hendrik exulted.

❧ CHAPTER TWENTY-FOUR ❧
Sunday evening, December 24, 1933

The East High *a cappella* choir performed at four different church services on Christmas Eve Day. Tom's voice was hoarse from the effort, but his unburdened heart sang. It began to snow as he walked home from the choir's final performance. A light dusting at first, the snowfall grew heavier until huge flakes spiraled down in the late afternoon sky, coating the barren trees and covering the sidewalks. *A white Christmas!* he thought with a thrill of pleasure.

All his senses seemed heightened, ratcheted up to superhuman sharpness. Though it was ridiculous, he thought he could actually *hear* the snow, each giant flake landing with a tiny splat as it melded to its fellows on the ground. The colors that splashed through the windows of the modest homes lining their street seemed brighter than normal, almost iridescent as they spilled into the night. His nostrils flared at the scents of dinner cooking in each house.

His mind drifted out and over the city. He *was* Santa. He could see through roofs and walls, watching parents bustle about in fevered preparations. His heart soared. The children were waiting for *him*. He could feel their eager anticipation, sense their wakefulness. Santa smiled to himself. He would wait until the young ones lost their battles with sleep, then slide noiselessly into their homes and leave wonderful surprises.

The images faded, and he was once again just Tom van Sloten, a former West Side boy from in between the tracks. Tingling with the vision's afterglow, he realized he hadn't once thought about what he himself wanted for Christmas. *Santa doesn't get presents!* he chuckled. He was out of money. Flat broke. The university was further away than ever. But it didn't matter. He was free and had never felt happier in his life.

Tom raced home, earthbound but brimming with joy. As he dashed up the steps, he admired the magnificent tree ablaze with lights and shimmering tinsel. The children had placed a small cardboard nativity scene under it.

After supper the family sang carols and Sarah read the Christmas story. The younger children hung their stockings on the mantel over the fireplace. Jean's gym sock was too large to hang, so she draped it over a chair. The boys insisted on leaving a plate of shortbreads and a tall glass of milk for Santa's traditional snack. Apples for his reindeer completed the small offering.

Tom picked up the two professionally wrapped presents he had hidden under the tree when his parents weren't looking. "Mom, this is for you," he said with obvious pride, handing his mother a mysterious package. "It's from all of us kids." An elegant bow and gold Rosenblatt stickers declared the gift's provenance.

Sarah opened it slowly, making the magic last.

"Oh!" she gasped, inhaling with surprise as she pulled out the new scarf and matching gloves. "They're—they're *beautiful!*"

"Try them on, Mom!" Richard urged.

Sarah draped the long scarf around her neck, relishing its soft feel as she admired herself in the mirror.

"Red's a wonderful color on you, Mom," Jean approved.

"I feel so—so, well, *elegant*," she murmured, overcome with the unexpected luxury.

The children clapped in delight as she hugged each one.

Tom waited until the hubbub subsided. "Dad, this is for you. From us," he said, handing his father a slim, elongated box. Hendrik was too astonished to speak. He removed the ribbon and stickers with great care, saving them for future Christmases. Then he swallowed with emotion as he lifted the lid and saw the Royal Stuart tartan tie nestled between layers of crisp tissue paper.

"I—I never thought I'd ever have one of these," he choked. He raised the tie for everyone to admire. "I'll wear it with honor and pride. And think of all you children every time I sing Scottish ballads and Harry Lauder songs!"

He put on the new tie, knotting it in a neat four-in-hand. He squared his shoulders and looked in the mirror. "I do look rather grand, don't I?" he grinned.

"Sing, Dad! Please sing us a song," Richard begged.

Henry never needed much prompting. He burst into a spirited rendition of the children's favorite Scottish folk tune, "Oh, I Hate to Get Up in th' Mornin'." Everyone laughed uproariously, giggling at the thick brogue the beloved song required for full dramatic effect. Hendrik didn't disappoint, affecting an even heavier accent than usual. Everyone joined in the chorus.

The last event on Christmas Eve was always the same. The children opened their gifts from their parents. The gifts were always the same too: new pajamas to replace last year's old ones.

Tom glanced sideways at Richard. His brother looked as though he was trying hard not to cry.

Jean broke in with forced cheerfulness. "I don't know about anybody else, but I'm worn out! I'm going to get into my new p.j.'s and get to sleep. Remember, Santa can't come while we're awake," she admonished the younger children with a wink.

Tom waited until everyone but Hendrik and Sarah had gone to bed. Then he slipped next door to retrieve his treasures. "Let's start with the stockings," he whispered as he carried in the bounty. Sarah and Hendrik put the oranges in first, filling out the toe of each sock. Then they added the nuts and candies. Tom hid the small gifts in each child's stocking, then topped them off with the giant candy canes. He even filled one for himself, smiling at his newfound subterfuge.

They stepped back and admired the bulging stockings.

Then it was time for the Santa Claus presents. Davey's blocks and Paul's refurbished train were laid out under the tree with a hand-lettered sign that marked each child's gift. Tom then positioned Jean's sweater set, trying with moderate success to duplicate the artistic arrangement he had seen in Rosenblatt's display case.

"Oh, Tom!" his mother breathed in delight. "It's gorgeous! Jeannie will be the best-dressed girl at her New Year's Eve party, I just know it!"

He saved the best for last. He pushed the bicycle into the living room and stood it on its kickstand next to the tree. It gleamed in the reflected lights. A cardboard tag hung from the polished chrome handlebars. It said simply, RICHARD. FROM SANTA.

In his final act as the substitute Santa, Tom ate the cookies, drank the milk, and took bites out of the apples. He hoped it looked like reindeer teeth had been gnawing on the fruit. He found a pencil stub and wrote a thank-you note, which he placed under the empty plate:

DEAR VAN SLOTEN CHILDREN,

YOU'VE BEEN VERY GOOD KIDS. THE BEST, I THINK.

KEEP UP THE GOOD WORK! MRS. C. AND I HOPE YOU LIKE THE GIFTS. SEE YOU NEXT YEAR!

LOVE,

SANTA

Hendrik hugged his weary son. "We're proud of you, Tom. For the man you're becoming, maybe all too quickly. For what you've done for the family. For your mother and me, this is the best Christmas ever!"

Tom gave his father a grateful smile, kissed his mother, and headed for the sleeping porch.

Hendrik and Sarah stood quietly for a moment, holding hands and admiring the tree, the bursting stockings, the array of gifts. Then Hendrik leaned forward. "Sarah?" he inquired, turning to his wife with a puzzled look. "What's that?" He pointed to a small rectangular package tucked in an out-of-the-way spot under the tree. It was wrapped in newspaper and tied with a frayed piece of twine. "I could swear it wasn't there earlier."

Sarah was as mystified as her husband. "I don't know, Henry. I've never seen it before. Maybe it's been there all the time and we just didn't notice?"

"I don't think so, Sarah," he said as he stared at the package. A small card was stuck under the string. "Should we?" He cocked an eyebrow at her.

Sarah grinned, "Snoop? Why not! After all, it's Christmas Eve. Go ahead, Henry. What does it say?"

Hendrik picked up the package and opened the card. A smile slowly spread across his face.

"Well," Sarah demanded. "What does it say? Who's it for? And who's it from?"

Henry turned the card toward her.

In simple block letters that betrayed no hint of authorship, the card read:

TOM. FROM SANTA.

Tom donned his new pajamas in the kitchen, steeling himself once again for the frigid sleeping porch. He took the usual deep breath, gritted his teeth, yanked the door open, and dived across the room into the bunk bed. As he lay there shivering, an unbidden thought crept into his consciousness. He felt the first stab of a new, adult anxiety that would remain with him for the rest of his life.

Would what he had done be enough?

Would the offerings be accepted?

❧ EPILOGUE ❧
Monday, December 20, 1992

This year it was Richard's turn to host the traditional van Sloten family Christmas supper. By the time the six brothers and sisters, spouses, grandchildren, married cousins and *their* children, plus a few guests and neighbors had squeezed in, Richard's spacious home in the foothills overlooking the city was overflowing. Excited chatter filled the "great room," where a fire crackled merrily in the wide stone fireplace.

A large Christmas tree stood in the corner next to a mound of gifts, its lights twinkling. Some of the old family ornaments, now faded and scratched with wear, had been hung on its bushy branches. Others had been made by the grandchildren. Some had been collected during Richard's frequent business trips to Europe and Asia.

Tom surveyed the gathering with a rush of nostalgia. It was the kind of gathering Hendrik and Sarah would have loved. He still missed them terribly, even after all these years. He wondered for the thousandth time if adequate medical care really could have alleviated Hendrik's congestive heart failure and lengthened his life. He sighed. The question was moot now.

After supper, Richard summoned the clan together. Following his welcome, a prayer and Christmas carols started the festivities.

Then he made a special family announcement. "Aunt Jean just learned

one of her newest poems will be published in the *Atlantic Monthly*."
Everyone applauded. They were all immensely proud of Jean, the family's
famous author and poetess. *And none of us even knew, not until she was well
into her thirties!* Tom recalled, amused at Jean's early and frequent use of
humorous pseudonyms.

Richard continued, "Instead of the usual program, Kate and I thought
that the children might be interested to hear their parents—some of the
aunts and uncles, that is—talk about their most memorable Christmas ever."
He suggested that the siblings tell their stories in reverse order of seniority.
Annie, the youngest, would be first, while Tom, the oldest, would speak last.

Everyone was spellbound as Annie, Dave, and Paul spoke.

Then it was Richard's turn. "My most memorable Christmas occurred
during the depths of the Depression," he began. "Annie wasn't even born
yet. I was only ten years old. Old enough to feel the concern and anxiety of
my parents, but too young to understand the constant worry of providing for
a large family in those difficult years. Dad had been out of work for a long
time, so we were really poor."

He paused, visibly struggling to contain his feelings. When he resumed,
a remarkable transformation had occurred. Richard was once again ten years
old, a child of the Great Depression.

The room was still.

"I had a secret wish that long-ago Christmas," he reflected. "I wanted a
bicycle. More than I'd ever wanted anything. It was an impossible dream.
Something that was so far beyond reason I scarcely dared even think about
it, let alone hope for such an extravagance.

"Christmas Eve came. After dinner, the kids opened the small gifts we
always made for each other. Tom had an after-school job at Rosenblatt's

Department Store, so he gave Grandmother Sarah and Grandpa Henry presents from all of us. If I remember right, Dad's gift was the old tartan tie that Tom still wears every Christmas."

Tom nodded as Richard continued.

"Then we opened our gifts from Mom and Dad. It was always the same every year. Pajamas. I remember trying really hard not to cry. Davey and Paul put out some cookies and milk for Santa. I didn't say anything, but I was sure Santa was going to skip our house that year."

Ten-year-old Richard's face was bleak as he struggled to keep his disappointment from showing.

"Dad always got up first on Christmas morning. He would stoke the coal fire and turn the tree lights on. Then, and only then, were we allowed to come into the living room. I knew in my heart of hearts that Santa hadn't come. The floor under the tree would be as bare as it had been the night before. But I wanted to be a 'good scout,' so I straightened up in my new pajamas and trooped in with the rest of the kids.

"When we walked in, I rubbed my eyes in disbelief. There—*there*, right next to the tree—was the shiniest, most beautiful bicycle I'd ever seen! And it had a great big tag on it that said, 'RICHARD'!"

He sat down and gulped back a sob, his voice still thick with wonder.

Tom's mind raced while Jean gave her account of that special Christmas. He was sorely tempted to tell the rest of the story. After more than half a century, what would it matter if he revealed the old secret? And in the process at long last got a little credit for his sacrifice?

Finally it was his turn. "That was my most memorable Christmas too," he began. He paused, still debating. Out of habit, he pulled out Hendrik's old pocket watch and glanced at it. Its thin silver plate was almost gone, rubbed down to the underlying brass. He had attached the watch to a gold chain that anchored his lifelong talisman, the double eagle coin. Absently he fingered the coin. The eagle was almost worn away, its fierce scowl softened with the years.

"I didn't expect to receive anything from Santa. But something really mysterious happened . . . I still think about it, even after all this time. I knew Mom and Dad didn't have any money. I know you can't imagine this, but sometimes we scarcely had enough to eat.

"You know how I love books," he continued, to no one's surprise. Tom had a large personal library and owned a prized collection of rare books. "Books. That's really all I ever wanted. And that very same Christmas Santa left me a First Edition I'd been dreaming about."

Tom glanced at Jean.

Her face was a studied blank, betraying nothing.

He fingered the frayed tartan tie. Hesitating a moment, he cleared his throat and resumed in a strong, steady voice.

"That book, Will Durant's *The Story of Philosophy,* is still my favorite. It made that Christmas my most memorable one ever."